Like Father...

...Like Son

Published by: Reading Stones Publishing
                  Helen Brown & Wendy Wood
                  Woodwendy1982.wixsite.com/readingstones
Cover Design: Wendy Wood

For more copies contact the publisher at:

Glenburnie Homestead
212 Glenburnie Road
ROB ROY NSW 2360
Mobile: 0422 577 663
Email: hbrown19561@gmail.com

Like Father...

...Like Son

Helen Brown

Reading Stones Publishing

1

Ben sat back in his chair. He smiled a self-satisfied smile. He had achieved what he wanted; he had taken over from his father, David. Yes, it had been by stealth and somewhere deep inside him, he knew that what he had done was wrong. He would have been here one day anyway, who cares how it happened.

His father only had himself to blame, every time, he, Ben, had made suggestions about changing things or doing things differently he would just tell him to be patient, he would be able to implement things when he was in charge, but right now he should be looking at how things work and maybe he might change his ideas later. It wasn't his fault that his father was taking too long to hand it over. He had tried to do things the nice way, by suggesting that his father retire early and spend more time with his mother, something he knew she had wanted, certainly when she was younger, however, over the years she had found ways to fill in the spare time that weighed on her with charity work.

He clearly remembered the moment that he had decided to try and dethrone his father. He had got bored sitting in his father's office at the age of ten and he had gone for a walk around the building. Harry, one of the business' board members, was in his office and Ben had wandered in and asked him what he did for his father. Harry had looked at him over the top of his glasses and said 'I'm the Chief Financial Officer and ideas man, the fuel if you like, that makes this ship run. I have ideas that will make it a good business, a better business, however, your father is at the steering wheel, and he turns it in the direction that he wants it to go. What this business needs is a man at the helm who will allow it to be the greatest business around. I hope that one day, you and I will be able to work together and turn this mighty ship around, but I guess I'll be too old for that by the time your father steps down.'

'But dad says I'll be here one day'

'Yeah, right!' the bitterness in Harry's voice was clear even to his ten-year-old's ears.

'Are you saying that he is lying to me?'

'Well, no, but he has changed over the years, and he wants to control everything himself and that will include you, my boy, take my word for it. You will just be his puppet even when he lets you work here.'

'But he said'.

'I know,' Harry sat thinking for a while, 'What is your favourite colour?' he asked with a glint in his eyes.

'Blue.' Ben shot back.

'I'll tell you what, you go and tell him that the walls of the office next to his would be nice if they were pale blue instead of that green, as it's going to be your office one day you should have a say in what colour it's going to be, and then come back and tell me what he says.'

Ben had done exactly what Harry had suggested and his father had looked at him as if he had two heads and told him there were more important things to spend money on. When Ben had returned to Harry's office, he gave him an "I told you so" look, and Harry suddenly seemed like his best mate. Over the months and years until he was eighteen, Ben had spent a lot of time in Harry's office and had soaked up every business idea that he fed him. That was where he had first laid eyes on Gloria. She had bounced into her father's office one day, wearing a very snug fitting light blue outfit. Ben was smitten at first glance. It was her seventeenth birthday, and Harry had casually dropped that information into the conversation and insisted that he and Gloria go out for lunch, his treat, in a classy restaurant that he knew she liked. It had given him a taste of the high life that he craved and after Gloria had told him that her father didn't really need to work because her parents had other streams of income making them independently wealthy, it occurred to him that by marrying Gloria he would have access to more of the same. He had pursued Gloria with determination from that day on, despite the objections of both his parents. They had married on her eighteenth birthday, Ben having just past his twentieth. That was just over a year ago.

6

Besides, Ben mused, there is a lot of prestige attached to being the youngest Chairman in the area, regardless of how you got there. There was a certain amount of satisfaction in seeing the look of surprise on his father's face when the board broke the news to him that he was being replaced by his own son. He hadn't visited his parents since that momentous board meeting when his coup had taken place. He didn't really want to see the look of disappointment that he knew would be on his mother's face. She was still a sweet woman with a heart of gold, and if he had any regrets at all, it was that she would be caught in the crossfire between him and his father.

2

The third anniversary of his take-over had arrived and Harry, Mavis, his wife, and Gloria would help him celebrate with dinner at his favourite restaurant in a couple of hours. He was going to meet them there, however, he suspected that they were more interested in celebrating the fact that Gloria was now six months pregnant, and they were going to be grandparents. Gloria was going to be a mother, the thought almost filled him with dread, as he had no idea how she would handle it.

They had married quickly, just a year from their first meeting. His father and mother had opposed the marriage. Maybe they were more intuitive than he was, but he had been determined to marry her; she was a large part of the scheme to dethrone his father. When he met her, she had been so charming, like his mother. Gloria had kept a lid on her demands until he had managed to unseat his father, then, once his position was secured in the business, another side of her nature became evident. She was still very charming in front of her parents, at functions, even in public, but at home, oh boy! nothing suited her. She was constantly needing new clothes and jewellery, the car upgraded, holidays, dinners at fancy restaurants, and if he said no, or even wait, there were tears, tantrums, days of sulking, and accusations about him not loving her enough. In short, she was a spoilt brat, but she was still the daughter of the most influential member of the board. He needed to keep Harry, on side if he was going to keep his position as Chairman. If Ben crossed him or made him cranky, he would turn on him, just as he had on his father. So, divorcing Gloria was not an option, at least not until his father-in-law was kind enough to die, but sadly, he was fairly young and in good health.

Despite all this though, he derived a great deal of satisfaction from knowing that Gloria was pregnant. She hadn't wanted children, and if he was honest, it was hard for him to make love to her after listening to her whinging most evenings. When they did make love, it had turned into a very stilted act, and she was always very careful to make sure that precautions were taken. It had taken some devious moves on his part, just like the moves he had made on his father, but the outcome was that she was with child, something he had wanted.

His In-laws had been nagging them for a grandchild for some time and he wanted an heir, partly to keep them happy and cement his position in the business, but also if he was honest, he wanted his wife to give him something he couldn't get himself and a child was the only thing that fitted the bill. His plan had been simmering around in his head for some time and he knew that he would have to be patient, but he would seize the opportunity when it arose.

Six months earlier, they were to attend a party. While they were getting ready, he noticed that Gloria had a new dress and when he asked her why she had bought it when there were so many new clothes in the dressing room, her response had simply been, because she wanted it. It was a figure-hugging red affair that he had to agree made her look very desirable. Blue might be his favourite colour but red on Gloria made her look stunning, as he had advanced towards her, with desire burning in his eyes, she giggled coyly at him and reminded him that those at the party were waiting for them. He felt the anger rising inside him, how dare she tease him like this and not give him the enjoyment that he wanted when he gave her so much. He pushed the anger down, tonight he would have his way, but he knew that he had to be careful, if he made a wrong move, his plan would come unstuck big time.

On the drive to the venue, he formulated his plan. They arrived at the party and Gloria worked the room, flirting with the men and being her most charming with the women. He made sure that the waiters keep her glass full, he wanted her well and truly mellowed with wine. He also moved around the room, keeping a very close eye on his wife without actually looking at her, pretending to drink but making sure he stayed stone-cold sober, he'd need his wits about him later.

When he was ready, he deliberately engaged his in-laws in conversation. He started to complain about a headache. He knew that Gloria wouldn't want to leave as they had been there only for a few hours, and the party would most likely go on into the early morning. He knew that he couldn't afford to look like they were being rude by just leaving but he was determined that they would be home earlier than usual. His In-laws had risen to the occasion superbly, insisting that they get a taxi to take he and Gloria home, after all, Gloria was way too drunk to be driving. He made suitable noises of regret but inside he was cheering. He had developed some serious acting skills over the years and now he played his script to an Oscar Award winning level. Being home after midnight was not what he wanted when he was planning to bed his wife against her wishes and so they left, albeit with Gloria moaning about not being able to stay. He had even managed to keep the act up until they had arrived home. Gloria was sulking, the way he knew she would, but once inside the door, she'd declared that she was going straight to bed. He indicated that he would stay downstairs for a while, making her feel safe to retire.

He silently climbed the stairs, discarding most of his clothes on the way up and walked into the bedroom, just as she was trying, fairly unsuccessfully, to remove her dress. His "headache" was gone and the anger he had felt earlier was again rising. Her protests lacked the intensity that he was expecting as he stepped up to help, the alcohol had reduced her normal defences and made her more responsive. His anger dissipated as he realised that she was actually giving him the come-on, so, it wasn't long before the hunger inside of him was satisfied. Since that night, if he wanted his needs met, making sure wine was on the table was the easiest way to achieve it.

Of course, she had been horrified when she discovered that she was actually pregnant, but the joy expressed by her parents and the pampering that she was given by other women in their circle, helped her to accept that she had to go through with it, however, the complaining at home was an even bigger issue now, which meant that he was often staying late at work in order to avoid the barrage that met him every night when he got home. The day she found out that she was carrying twins would go down in their history as the night when she really created a scene. It was a wonder the neighbours hadn't called the police on them. She was now six months pregnant, and her doctor had a policy of not revealing the gender of the babies, claiming that the scans were too unreliable, so they would have to wait until they were born to find out if they were having two boys, two girls, or one of each. He was hoping for a boy and a girl.

****

Ben sat back; the food had been very enjoyable as always; they had dined here so many times that they were on a first name basis with the staff and owners. So, why was he suddenly overcome with this strong feeling of dreariness? He had stopped listening to his in-laws going on again about how they were going to enjoy being grandparents and all the things they were going to spoil the babies with. What was happening to him? Not that many years ago, he had strived so hard to be in this position, yet here he was, sitting in his favourite restaurant, in an expensive suit, having driven here in a Bentley, and suddenly, he was aware that not only was he bored but this lifestyle had lost its lustre. There had to be more to life than the accumulation of things, power, and prestige. Suddenly he realised that his parents had had a better quality of life when he was a baby without all the trapping that he had. Maybe he was starting to grow up somewhat. There was one big problem for him though, he couldn't, or wouldn't, just walk away from this life, that to some extent, he realised was being forced on him by his father-in-law. *I'm like a bird trapped in a large, gilded cage. I'm free to move around as long as I only flutter between the office, home, and these sorts of functions. If I really wanted to spread my wings and do something completely new there would be just no way that would be allowed. What would he do? If he was free of this cage he was in, what new venture would he tackle?* With suddenly clarity he realised that it would probably be much the same thing as he was doing now, it's just being locked in this rut that had him so down. He loved the business, negotiating deals and the satisfaction of seeing signed contracts on his desk. It was more the idea of having the freedom to say no occasionally that appealed to him but with Harry's control the way it was, it just didn't seem possible. Would there ever be a time when he could have both the good things that came with this lifestyle as well as those things that he now knew that people like his parents had.

'Ben are you alright?' Mavis asked quietly.

'Yeah, I'm just feeling tired. It's been a big week'. He smiled wanly at his mother-in-law. She never said much, but just now, he had the feeling that this woman kept her finger on the pulse of things more that anyone gave her credit for but then he dismissed it as being unlikely.

The twins, a girl, and a boy, now fifteen, had arrived safely and they had named the boy John which was Harry's middle name. They had thought about naming him Harry, but he had to work with his father-in-law and having two Harry's could create confusion. The girl was given the name Elizabeth. Although it was his own mother's name, it was also Mavis' middle name making it easier to pretend that the twins had been named only after that side of the family, looking as if Ben's family were cut out of the picture all together.

Gloria took to motherhood much better than he had hoped. Yes, she had demanded that servants were employed, but she had stopped nagging him about having the house updated every few months. Instead, what she required were things for the kids, but he was happy to indulge them rather than Gloria. He had no plans to bring John into the business, after all, that was how he had learnt the skills to upstage his father and he wasn't taking the risk of John being able to do the same. He was planning on being the Chairman for a very long time and keeping John away from the business was going to ensure that would happen. John hadn't shown any interest in the business anyway, he was quite happy to reap the rewards of being a successful businessman's son and make the most of the good life that it provided.

****

David watched as the two young people walked in his direction. It didn't take long for him to get a fair idea as to who they were. A lump formed in his throat. It was as if Beth was walking towards him, just as she had so many times when they were at school together. He shook his head as if to clear it. It couldn't be, Beth had been gone for more than two years now and she had been a mature woman when that had happened, but the girl was the spitting imagine of her. She had the same beautiful features, light brown hair and high cheek bones, of her grandmother, sadly, he noted that she didn't quite have the same gentle look about her, there was a hardness in her eyes that affected her face and most likely her attitude. The young lad, well, he was tall and had a familiar look too, that of his father. He had a swagger that spoke of cockiness rather than confidence and an arrogance about him that made David feel afraid and sad at the same time. Deep down inside him, he knew these two were his grandchildren. He had not met them; they had been born after his son had cut ties with him, but he knew who they were.

They probably wouldn't even see him. As a homeless person, he was invisible. They would most likely just walk past and not even look in his direction, but he couldn't help but stare at them.

What happened next would confuse and hurt so badly. The young man, David didn't even know his name, spotted him looking their way.

'What are you looking at old man?', the tone of his voice was so spiteful, as if he didn't deserve to be alive.

'I'm just thinking what a fine strong man you are', David replied, 'what's your name?'

'John, why would you want to know?', John was looking closer at the man in disgust. David knew that he seriously needed to have a bath and some clean clothes, but he wasn't comfortable with the way John was looking at him.

'And the young lady, is she your sister?', David ploughed on, trying to ignore the strange stares they were both giving him now.

'Yeah, what made to say that, how did you know she would be my sister and not my missus?' John's tone was puzzled and had a hard edge to it.

Suddenly, John's face lit up, but not in a friendly way. The look was harder than ever and there was a very nasty glint in his eyes that made David even more afraid.

John elbowed his sister. "You know who this is?" he smirked.

'No.' the girl looked at the old man and then at her brother.

'It's Pop I reckon, Dad's father.'

'You're joking, right?' the girl replied, 'He's been here all the time?'

'It looks like it, Dad won't be pleased at all. He was hoping that he was dead. He didn't want him around to cause any trouble.'

The look of hatred on John's face made fear grip David all over. His son had not only taken the business from him but had eventually left him homeless. It now appeared that David's prayers for his son had not yet been answered.

'Well ....., we might have to see what we can do about this. I need to get back into dad's good books after putting that dint in the car last week.' John snarled at David.

'What are you going to do, you can't kill him, John?' the girl gripped his arm, fear showed in her voice as well. David felt a small seed of relief grow, there was some of Beth in there after all.

'Oh, Liz, stop it, I won't kill him, but I'm going to make sure that he is put away for good so he cannot create any bother.'

What happened after that was like watching a play in slow motion but happened so quickly that David's head was left spinning.

John looked around as if to check that no one was watching and then turned to Liz, come on sis, I want you to bash me up. Punch me, just like we used to do as kids. Pull my hair, come on kick me. This has got to look real. Liz looked at her brother, a look of anticipation came over her face, she was going to enjoy this, even in his confusion, David could see that.

'What are you doing, stop this.' David pleaded?

'Shut up old man!' John spat at him.

David watched in horror as John and Liz started to kick and scratch each other. Suddenly John produced a knife from somewhere and came towards David. David pulled back but John grabbed his hand and wrapped it around the handle. Shoving David back against the wall John took the knife and stabbed himself. David gasped. The wound wasn't

15

deep and wouldn't be life threatening but what was going on, David had no idea. Then John stepped back a few places, he made eye contact with David, with a brief grin on his face, John dropped the knife in front of him and fell dramatically to the ground, screaming for help as his did so.

In the confusion that followed as staff from a nearby shop rushed out to see what was going on, David registered that Liz had disappeared. She must have run off once John had produced the knife, it would have been her cue to leave.

John was pointing to David, 'He attacked me' his voice was suitably soft to appear weak.

The police arrived and David was bundled into the van. David glanced back at John who was now sitting up with a self-satisfied smirk on his face. They arrived at the nearest station a few minutes later.

He was put in a cell before he really knew what was happening. David looked at the name on the officer's badge as he was escorted to the cell. There was something familiar about this man and the name, but he couldn't think why that would be. As he sat down on the bench-come-bed, he thought, *how did this happen? Well at least I'll be safe tonight.*

He lay down and let his memories drift into focus.

> David looked down at his baby son. The pride and love that surged through him felt almost painful. All he had ever wanted was to be a father, a good father, at that. It was a desire that he'd nurtured since he was about ten years old.
>
> Some people might say that at ten, a person was too young to know what they wanted to do but he had, and it had remained number one over everything else on his priority list.
>
> The baby's chubby red face, his ten fingers, his long eyelashes and small body all wrapped up in his blanket just melted his heart. He gently lifted him from the arms of his wife and sat in the chair over next to the window of the

hospital room. He stared at him for such a long time, or so it seemed. What those around him didn't know was that deep in his heart David was making the biggest commitment of his life. He wasn't saying anything out loud, but he prayed, 'Lord, help me to raise this child, to give him the very best tools to make the most of his life so that he will honour you and so will I'. He didn't only pray this once but over, and over again as if by repeating it, it would be imprinted on his heart permanently.

His son opened his eyes, they were blue, he squirmed a little and started to cry. David looked at his wife, she had drifted off to sleep and stirred at the sound. She smiled at them both, 'He's probably getting hungry, you'd better give him here so I can feed him', her voice sounded tired but filled with love.

'Alright, I'd better get back to work then, the business won't look after itself all of the time, I'll call back later tonight before I go home,' he said, a wistful note in his voice. Part of him wanted to stay and watch them for hours, drinking in the beauty of them both. The other part was keen to get started on the challenge that he had just set himself while he was holding his son.

It wasn't that he hadn't worked hard up until now, he had, and it was always to make sure that his child would have a great start in life and a business that would give him a wonderful lifestyle as an adult.

He drove back to the office. He parked the car in his specially marked parking bay. He got out, locked the car, and headed to the office. He felt like he was walking on air.

He rode the elevator with a smile from ear to ear. As he approached his secretary, Mavis', desk she looked up, 'Well, what did you have?' she asked.

'It's a boy!' he smiled, 'A beautiful baby boy.'

'Congratulations,' she responded, as she returned to her work.

David walked into his office, sat down at his desk but all he could do was spin his chair around and around. He just could not focus.

He thought back to the day he had decided that he wanted to be a father. His father was so busy at work that they didn't spend very much time together as a family. His childhood had been a lonely one.

During his tenth year his family had gone to visit his mother's sister, Jane and her husband, Ben. Their baby son had been born a few months earlier. Visiting family, or anyone for that matter, was a rare event, so rare in fact that it was one of those things that was indelibly imprinted in David's memory.

When they arrived, there was a lot of fuss made of the baby, but it wasn't long before he had been put down in the bassinet and the men had gone outside. Mum had gone into the kitchen to help Aunty Jane.

David had been left to his own devices. He had wandered around the room wondering what to do with himself. The bassinet was set up near the window. He went over to look at the baby. Patrick was lying there and looked at David as he peered over the edge. He had smiled, David had reached in to pat him, and the baby had grabbed his finger. Patrick started making cute sounds and David understood that he was trying to talk to him even if he didn't understand anything that he was saying. His Aunty returned to the room.

'Hey there, you're talking to Patrick, he likes you,' His Aunt's voice was filled with joy, love, and warmth. She had placed her arm around his shoulder and given him a hug. He had watched Jane and Ben while they had been showing off their baby. Their happy smiles, the happiness that surrounded them and filled the house, was something that David didn't have at home, and he wanted it so bad.

One day, he vowed quietly to himself, he was going to be a father and he would have a nice loving family just like this one. Now his dream had come true. He had a wife who loved him, more than that she made sure that his life at home was ordered and she had a happy smile most of the time.

There had been some days when it had faded quite a bit while she was suffering from morning sickness, but Beth's smile had returned, he had seen it when she woke up in the hospital room. His wife had already agreed to name their son, Ben, after his uncle; if it had been a girl, her name would have been Jane but in his hearts of hearts he really wanted a boy, now his son was here. Life was so good.

David looked at the clock. It was five O'clock already. He hadn't done anything since he had arrived back at the office earlier this afternoon. His secretary had been right, he should have taken the whole day off instead of just the morning. Oh well, he thought he might as well get some tea at the café down the street and then go back to see Beth and the baby. Tomorrow was another day but after a night's sleep he would be in a better mood to pull himself into gear and get on with his work.

4

While some people would describe David's life growing up as difficult, others might consider isolated a better description.

His father had worked long hours. As he grew older, David was to discover that, while he worked hard during the day, many of his hours after work were spent at the pub or club either at the bar or in front of the poker machine. Weekend hours were often spent at the racetrack, betting on horses or greyhounds. However, as a child he believed what his father told him and therefore he was convinced that it was work that occupied so much of his father's time.

It wasn't that he was a mean father, he just wasn't there. They didn't starve, he wasn't careless with his money, it was more a matter of socialising that kept him frequenting these venues. He convinced himself that he was building business connections. More astute folks knew that he just had a need to be seen as being more successful than was an actual reality. His mother had to do everything, maintaining the house, gardening, cleaning, cooking, and washing was her domain, not because she wanted it that way, but by default due to an absent husband.

As a child, of course, David had no idea that this was unusual, his mother didn't tell him that things should or could be different. Maybe she was too busy or just reluctant to discuss adult issues with a mere child. Whatever her reasoning, he grew up in ignorance.

It also meant that the older he got, the greater the workload became for him in order to help his mother. He learnt how to mow the lawn, fix a tap, take out the rubbish, dig a garden and a list of numerous other things that would help ease his mother's load resulting in a physical development that was above average for his age group.

This also meant that the family had a very limited social life. The lack of social involvement did nothing to broaden David's knowledge of what might be or even what realities existed for those who lived outside the four walls of his home. He also developed an ability to work alone and found that he didn't need the company of others to be content.

Even at school, boy talk, what little talk there was, did not centre around the workings of home-life, but was more inclined to be about the adventures to be had, tracking animals or the marvels of machines that would one day create a world where leisure would be the predominate activity of all mankind, replacing the hard day to day slog of back-breaking work that currently existed.

He wasn't a particularly bright boy, but what he lacked in natural ability he made up for with determination. He had to work hard, and he gave it his all to make progress, finding that mathematics was the subject that engaged him the most. Reading, while requiring a moderate effort, was generally restricted to business and economic materials, all in preparation for his working life once his school days were behind him.

He was bright enough, even at an early age, to realise that in order to make a greater success of his life he would have to concentrate his efforts along a limited pathway. A narrow channel moved water much faster than a wide one.

****

David's teacher insisted that Elizabeth Jones sit next to him in class, she was a quiet, unassuming child, and even at that young age, pretty to look at, not that David would admit it to anyone, not even to himself. Somehow, the teacher knew that her exceptional skills in writing would add a broader base to David's skill set and that he could help her to improve her number skills, the subject that he knew she struggled with. Looking back, David saw that the teacher had done this deliberately, he largely left them to get on with their work, making sure that they had plenty to do. Many of the other children needed to be constantly reminded to stay focused, something that Elizabeth and David didn't. With all the jobs that he needed to help his mother with once he got home, David made sure that his schoolwork was up to date before the bell rang each day to indicate that time was up. He would often return to the classroom after he had finished his lunch in order to finish some uncompleted project. This friendship was to last all the way through school and into their college years. David couldn't really remember when he fell in love with Elizabeth, looking back it was probably something that grew slowly over time, starting with that first day when the teacher had told her to move her books and sit beside him. During the last couple of months, leading up to their last day at college, David started to think about what life would be like without seeing Elizabeth every day. He knew that it was something that he didn't like or want. He had been working during the weekends and any days that didn't require him to be on campus, so he was fortunate to have some money saved. One night, while they were walking home, they had passed a jewellery store. There was a new display in the window with some very flashy rings and watches. Elizabeth had stopped, telling David that she would never wear such a large creation, she pointed to one at the back, which had a narrow, modest band and a small diamond set in a simple setting. 'If I had a choice, I would pick that one over this one in the front,' she had said wistfully. Was she hinting that she wanted their relationship to go to the next level? David had the feeling that she was, and it boosted his courage. A couple of days later, he entered the store, asked about the ring Elizabeth had pointed out and found that it was well within his means to purchase, which he did. They picnicked the following Sunday, a thing that they often did, giving Elizabeth no hint of the surprise, he was about to spring on her.

'Have you decided yet, what you are going to do when college is finished?' David had asked, knowing that she had a few offers she had been considering.

'Not, yet. The Brown & Smith offer is the one I'm leaning towards. You?'

'Yes, I've decided to take the job I've been offered with Mr Standford. I think I can learn a great deal from him.'

'Brown & Smith is just around the corner.'

'Hmm, sounds like we are still going to be able to see each other then.' David said, watching her carefully and noticing that the light in her eyes started to fade. He had to stop teasing her, or he was going to lose her forever, if he wasn't careful. 'Elizabeth, where are you planning on living then?'

'I'll have to find a flat somewhere, they are expensive down there, but it's too far to travel from Mum and Dad's every day.'

'What if we shared a flat?'

'David, what are you saying, you know that we can't… not as single people, it's not done.' David reached into his pocket, bringing out the ring case and opening it, 'Then, would you please do me the honour of becoming my wife. I want to see you every day, wake up with you beside me in the mornings from here on.'

'Oh, yes. Yes, David I would love to be your wife.' He lent in and kissed her. They had married quickly. Despite the fact that friends and even family had accused them of it being a shotgun one, Ben hadn't arrived until five years later. They had both worked hard, soon buying their own house because neither of them could see them being able to raise a family in the small space they were living in. They had always planned to have more than one child, but things didn't work that way, Ben ended up being an only child.

No one realises just how much one small person can so completely change your life until it happens. The lack of sleep that happened every night, not just now and again, but every single night took its toll and was something that no-one could tell you about. David could see the exhaustion on Beth's face at the end of each day when he arrived home. The house wasn't as spotless as it was before what David called "Benflux". He made up the word because there had been such an influx of good things and new challenges that David said the word "Benflux" was fitting. Even so, David couldn't wait to get home after work each day. He would sit and cuddle his son until it was necessary for Beth to give him a feed. He even took turns in changing his nappies, despite the unpleasantness of the task but he wanted to be involved in his son's life, not just the good bits but the messy stuff as well.

He relished the smiles that he gave, talked to him constantly and even read stories to him. Life was good and David was making the most of it.

Around the time that Ben started to walk, he worked even harder at the office. He wanted to make sure that the business would be strong for Ben to take over one day. His father had worked long hours and was too focused on wanting things to suit him. David didn't want to go down that road. He tried to make sure that he was home no later than eight at night. He lifted his standards and expected his staff to do the same. He didn't realise that he was starting down a very dangerous road, something that he swore he would never do. He was to discover later that these things happen by degrees, very slowly. While he was a good father at home, he was becoming more demanding at work. Most people have dual personalities, the good and the bad.

The weekends were taken up with teaching Ben all the things that David felt that he would need to survive in the cutthroat world of business. It never occurred to him that Ben might not want to follow in his father's footsteps. Ben followed his father everywhere as a child and David assumed that was the way it was always going to be.

As a pre-schooler, Ben used to love going into the office with David when on the few occasions he needed to catch up on a Saturday morning. He would walk around David's office, running his hands over the furniture, looking as if he envied his father for being able to work there. As soon as he could talk, he asked question after question. The boy seemed a natural. Once he was at school, he spent most of his school holidays in the office.

While Ben was at school, he tried out his skills by setting up his own little businesses, such as selling homemade lemonade on a stall from the driveway. He would take an extra lunch to school and sell it to the highest bidder. Of course, nether Beth nor David knew about the school escapades.

David, sitting in the cell, realised that it was during Ben's early teen years that things started to take a turn towards the maliciousness that led to where he now found himself.

He hadn't realised, that what he thought was Ben's appetite for the business, was hiding a greater desire to take over and outdo his father. Why or what had sparked the craving still wasn't clear to David. Had he been too busy to see what was happening right under his nose or was he just clueless.

David searched his memory banks trying to see what it was that had sparked Ben's mission. There were no friends that he knew of that could have steered Ben in the wrong direction. However, David realised now, way too late, that he didn't really know who Ben's friends were, let alone what influence they had on his son. Beth had shown concern a few times, but David had brushed them off as her being overprotective.

Oh, wow, I really didn't listen to her at all. How lonely her life must have been during those years? It's more than amazing that she was still so very gracious to me when Ben made his move on the business and tossed us out. She happily went back to work to make sure that we could eat. However, I guess that she probably had better company at work than she had at home. I really was that busy. When did I lose sight of the prayer that I prayed the day Ben was born?

With sudden clarity he realised that God hadn't allowed these things to happen to him, he had brought them on himself. He had pushed God out of his life and God had given him the freedom to do what he wanted but it also meant that he was now dealing with consequences of that freedom.

He hadn't deliberately pushed God away. It wasn't like he had stood up one day and said "God, get out of my life." It had happened by degrees, one half step at a time. There was the first night when he had decided that he didn't have time to read Ben a story book, to pray with him when he put him to bed. That one-off night had turned into more nights. The occasional night working back late turned into working back late nearly every night. It had taken years for the habit to develop but David realised that it had happened, and that most likely Ben resented the lack of attention. Had he been too naïve to think that his son would end up hating him so much. Beth had tried to warn him, but he wasn't listening, that was obvious. *Well, I've now got myself into a pretty pickle, how do I get myself out of this mess.*

5

Once the twins had arrived, it become clear to Ben that Harry really had no interest in him as a person, he was just a puppet. Harry still knew what strings to pull, and Ben didn't have the courage to stand up to him because if he did, he would make sure that Gloria found out and that would always cause problems at home. Ben admitted sometimes that he was getting very tired of the Harry games.

There was a spare office in the building, it was the one that Harry had indicated would be his when he started at the business, but he had managed to unseat his father without occupying it. He had used a similar office next to Harry's without his father being fully aware that was where he spent most of his time. He now wondered if it could be put to better use. It was helpful that it had an access door to his office. Maybe if he locked the door to the hallway, he could convert it into a small sitter, with a pull-out bed. That way he could spend some nights here in the building rather than go home and face the same music every night and maybe find some comfort as well. There were a couple of women in the office who he knew would be willing to give him what he wanted. The twins were now in their teens and the noise they created was annoying. They fought constantly which was nothing new, once, when they were smaller, Ben had come home to find them scrapping on the floor. When he had tried to separate them, Gloria had told him to let them be as they were only playing, but boy it had looked very nasty to him. However, he had given authority to Gloria, and he wasn't going to argue with her, it just wasn't worth the bother. As long a Gloria didn't complain to her father about him working too hard, it would work, but he'd have to be careful. One whiff of a scandal and he would be in trouble. There had to be a way to make it work, even if it was only now and again, just to give him a break.

He went to the pub across the street to have a couple of drinks before he went home. He couldn't afford to have more; he needed his wits about him more now than ever before. If he was too mellow, he was likely to give in to Gloria's demands without carefully weighing up the financial consequences, and she was trying to spend more and more money. He had made his bed, and even though it was extremely uncomfortable, he had to stay in it for the moment. If only his in-laws would disappear for a while or forever. The more he thought about this, though, the more he realised that Harry was the problem, and he really still did love Gloria, he just wished that she would go back to being the woman that he first met. Yes, things were hard and had he been able to make the choice years ago, he would've walked away. In that moment, he resolved to stay faithful to her for long as it took.

6

Early the next morning, having slept better than he had in years, David woke as he heard someone approach his cell. You become very sensitive to noise very quickly once you start living on the streets. The door of the cell opened. The Police Officer, who had taken his name at the desk when he had been brought in, seemed nice enough and was standing in the doorway. He was most likely about ten years younger than David.

'Ok, sir, you need to come with me', the officer said.

'Are you letting me go?' David asked.

'No, sorry sir, don't tell anyone but I have arranged for you to have a shower and there are some clean clothes from the lost property box for you to put on. You look as if it's been a while. I'm sure it will make you feel a bit better.'

'Oh, thank you sir, it certainly has been a while,' David smiled. He went to shake the officer's hand, but his hand stayed by his side.

'Come on, this way please.' The officer indicated that David should walk in front of him to a small room just around the corner. There was a toilet and a shower. It must have been available for the staff to use if they got messy in the line of duty. There was a towel, which had seen better days and clean clothes sitting on a bench. Soap and shampoo, the sort that you find in Motel rooms was also there. He was pretty sure that what wasn't used would be thrown in the bin afterwards.

'Please don't take too long. I have other duties to get on with', the officer seemed a bit nervous, so David got on with it. As much as he would've loved to stay there and just soak up the hot water and let it wash away the years of dirt and degrading lifestyle, he knew that time was of the essence.

Still, he relished the feel of clean clothes and freshly washed hair, even if it was much longer than he would have liked. It was now clean and that was to be enjoyed.

David was quickly returned to his cell. As the door clanged shut behind him, he smiled. A verse in the Bible came to mind. He couldn't remember where to find it, but he remembered what it said. "But as for you, ye thought evil against me; but God meant it unto good,". Yes, John had meant evil but here he was now with clean clothes, a roof over his head and four walls to protect him for the first time in a very long-time and that was good. Thank you, Lord, David breathed a prayer of thanks. His future was still uncertain, but tonight he would sleep better even than he had last night.

He laid back down on the bench provided, it was hard, but it felt luxuriously soft compared to concrete beds that had been his for the months he had been homeless.

As he laid there looking at the ceiling, the memory of his visit to his aunt and uncle's when he was ten years old kept playing on a loop around in his head. Why now? Why did that memory keep coming back to haunt him, today of all days? He had failed as a father and the dream that had been born that day had become a nightmare.

Uncle Ben, his parents didn't talk about them very much and when they did it was just Ben and Jane. They had never visited them again. He didn't even know what their surname was or if they were still alive for that matter. It had never occurred to him to go and visit them himself, which now seemed strange considering the fire that they had started in him at such a young age, maybe he had been more like his father than he wanted to admit even back then.

Oh, God, why are you torturing me? I know I have failed you and myself.

He spent the day, with his memories, no one disturbed him except to push his meals through the slot in the door.

****

When Ben got home on Monday night, he was surprised to find both his children seated at the table waiting for their evening meal. Usually, one or both would be hiding in their room, or they would be in front of the tv, eating.

He joined them at the table and started to eat. Things were very quiet for the first ten or fifteen minutes. When suddenly Liz, spoke to her father.

'Hey, dad. We went over to Lillydale yesterday. We were having a look around the shops while mum was at the beauty spar. There were a lot of homeless people in the mall.'

'I hoped you stayed away from them. Those people are just lazy bums, and they should just get a job.'

Liz looked at John and smiled.

'There was this one guy, we didn't get very close' John spoke with a cheeky tone in his voice, 'I swear, Dad, it could have been you, only older.'

'Do you think it might have been your dad?' Liz asked,

'Maybe,' Ben answered thoughtfully, 'I hope not, I don't want him coming back into my life and causing trouble again.'

'Oh, I doubt if he will be any trouble,' John said triumphally.

'What do you mean?' Gloria asked, 'how can you be so sure?'

'We saw him being carted away by the police, after he attacked some kid.'

'Humm well let's hope they lock him up and throw away the keys then.' Ben muttered, 'now let's not be bothered with the dregs of society and finish our meal.' Ben wasn't going to let on to his kids, but the mention of his father had dragged up some very unsettling feelings.

That night he lay awake for a long time. Something in what the kids had said or maybe it was the way they said it, worried him. They were fifteen now, John hadn't seemed at all remorseful when he had damaged his car last week and now, they were wondering around malls aimlessly, what were they going to do with the rest of their lives. If they had time to walk around checking out homeless people in the mall of Lillydale then they had too much time on their hands, also something he had overheard at work was adding fuel to his worries. He had heard members of the staff taking about a disturbance at the mall, but when one of them noticed him in the vicinity the conversation had shut down and everyone went back to their desks. He had assumed that it was because they had been talking in a group instead of working, but now he wondered if it might have been John and Liz that they had been talking about. He might not have spent a lot of time with his kids over the years but something in the way John told that story tonight didn't seem right; there was more to it, of that, he was sure. It was time those kids had something else to do other than follow their mother around. They needed to learn how to work. How he was going to make that happen without upsetting either Harry or Gloria he didn't know but he had to make it happen and the sooner the better. Of course, once one went to work, the other would follow but he had no idea how to get them into the workforce without upsetting the status quo. He needed to talk to some of his mates to see if they would give John and Liz work after school, besides, those two needed to spend some time apart from each other in order to learn how to stand on their own two feet. He'd need all the negotiating skills that he had ever developed to get this done.

****

David woke after a reasonable night's sleep. On one hand, he'd felt safer than he had for the last two years. Sleeping on the streets was fraught with danger, particularly at night but on the other hand his sleep had been haunted with dreams of his failures. He ate the breakfast that was pushed through a slot in the door to a small shelf inside the cell. If he was going to get good square meals like that, he was happy to stay put for as long as they would allow.

Hours passed and his life story continued to rotate around and around in his head.

It must have been getting toward mid-afternoon when he heard the lock on the door starting to work. They were such noisy things. Metal scraping against metal.

There was a loud clash as the lock on the cell door released. One of the Police Officers who had brought him to the station stood to one side. You're a lucky man he said, this man here says he is a relative of yours and so you can leave, as long as you stay in his care. I suggest that you be on your best behaviour. We talked to one of the shop owners near where the incident happened, and they backed your story that the attack on the young man was staged. I guess they didn't realise they were being watched. It's getting late, come back in tomorrow and we will discuss what happens next.

The Officer, who had arranged for him to shower and clean up, stepped forward. He was now dressed in jeans, a polo shirt and denim jacket.

'Sir, I'm Patrick Hartigan, your mother and my mother were sisters.'

'How do you know? I haven't seen you since you were a few months old.'

'I checked you out, so come with me and I'll give you a lift home.'

They reached a car parked in the lot. Patrick opened the door for David as if he was someone important. They drove in silence while Patrick manoeuvred the vehicle out of the lot and onto the main street and headed towards the south edge of town. It wasn't a big place, but it was big enough for people to maintain personal space. Unlike small places where everyone knew all your business, true or untrue.

'I'm surprised you knew I even existed. Mum and Dad never talked about your family, even after that visit. Gee that was fifty years ago!'

Patrick laughed, 'Don't remind me, I'm fifty years old and starting to feel it. Particularly when I have to chase down offenders. Mum and dad talked about you a lot, particularly after Aunt Susan died. One of mum's favourite memories was walking into the room when you visited them and seeing you talking to me. She felt that some sort of dream had been born that day, she used to say, "I saw it in his eyes". They always felt sorry for your mother and you as a kid but were so proud of what you achieved. Dad kept track of what you were doing and how you were getting on. We're nearly there, my wife has a cooked up a storm in your honour'

'Honour,' David almost sneered, 'I'm no one to be honoured. I'm just a homeless bum.'

'Not anymore', Patrick returned. 'We have a granny flat that Jo's mother used until she died two years ago, and Jo insists that you use it. She asked the Lord about renting out after her mother died and she was certain that He said "No, your family will need it on Tuesday". She told me that she had that thought three times that day. It was a puzzle to her as she has no family left. She was an only child like me. But, for the last two years she has vacuumed and made up the bed every Tuesday morning just in case. Every Wednesday she stripped the bed and put the sheets back in the cupboard. So today when I came home and told her that I had checked you out and that you were my cousin, she said that she'd finally had her answer.'

Wow, I've been homeless for two years. God had a home prepared for me and I didn't even know it.

'Wow, that's obedience in the extreme,' he said out loud.

'Well, she did say when I told her that I had found you that she nearly didn't do it this morning. Then she remembered the Bible story of the ten virgins and how five were prepared and five weren't. So, the flat is freshly vacuumed, and the bed is ready for you,' Patrick said as he pulled into the driveway of a well-maintained modest house. It was a white weather board home, with green trims, two leadlight panels either side of a matching door made for a very pretty entrance, giving the house what most people would have called a calm, neat curb appeal. They both got out of the car, David looked at Patrick across the roof.

'You got kids?' David asked, his voice sounding harsher than he meant.

'Nope, it just wasn't meant to be. It was hard on Jo, but she eventually found other things to fill in the emptiness. She cared for her mother for nearly ten years and found that easier without having to juggle children as well. God knew what we didn't.' They walked into the house, Patrick stepping to one side to allow David to move through the entrance way in front of him calling out as he did so.

'Jo, we're home.'

The lady that came into view, was short and plump, but her face lit up with the most beautiful smile.

'Welcome, David, it is so nice to finally meet you. Come on through and I'll show you your new home.' She turned and walked back the way she had come. David didn't move until Patrick gently prodded his back, nodding when David looked back at him. He followed Jo, as she walked into the kitchen, she turned right towards a door. The smells of a roast dinner assailed his senses. Oh, how long has it been since he had a proper cooked meal. Beth hadn't been able to cook once she got sick and his efforts never managed to match her cooking. Tears came to his eyes. Jo had stopped, her hand on the handle.

'David, are you alright' she asked, concern written all over her face. He nodded and she opened the door. 'This is your new abode' she said leading the way through a laundry. 'We share the laundry. You can do your own, I'll show you how to work the machine later.' She wasn't going to pamper him, by the sounds of it. Beth had been one to spoil him up until she had returned to work after Ben had taken everything from them. Even then she had done more than her fair share of the housework, he realised, adding another blot to his already long list of crimes. Jo had moved into a small sitting room with a kitchenette along one wall. It was a beautifully laid out room, with carpet, a couch, and a small table. David stopped.

'What do you people want from me for all of this?'

'Nothing, it is a place where you can stay and be warm and safe.' Patrick replied.

'I can't stay here. This is too much. I don't deserve this.'

'David, we are not allowing you stay here because you deserve this, you are family, and this is where you belong. All you have to do is be part of our family.'

'But, why? My own son threw me out, he deceived me and took all that I had. I must have done something really wrong for him to hate me that much.'

'David, I don't think it was you he hated, I think that it was his love for power and more money that took over his life. You and Beth were just collateral damage in the same way that drugs cause people to behave in unnatural ways, so power and greed cause others to disregard those they should be taking care of. Remember, God has the same problem. He just gets to see the why and the how, we don't,' David looked at Patrick, a puzzled expression on his face.

'What do you mean?'

'Well, people hurt God all the time, they take His good gifts and ruin them, use them to get what they want. Unlike you and Ben, where you don't understand what made him do what he did, God sees the triggers and the desires that get people into so much trouble. He is still watching Ben, and the children. You know that don't you?'

'Come on, it's time we ate,' Jo said. 'Tomorrow is Patrick's day off. So, he will take you shopping for some new clothes before you have to go back to the station. In the meantime, I've left you a pair of Patrick's pjs for tonight, just as well you are similar in size.'

They said down at the table in the main house, Patrick said grace after Jo had placed plates of food on the table. David could not remember when he last saw that much food.

7

As David lay in the bed that night, sleep evaded him once again. The generosity of these people was just too great to comprehend.

Why would they do this, there must be a price for me to pay. I must have to do something.

Their grace is a lot like mine.

David sat up in bed.

'Who said that?' He looked around the room, the full moon shining through the large window allowed him to see reasonably well; nothing seemed different, there certainly wasn't anyone in the room that was for sure. *Being homeless for so long must have sent me mad.* He lay down again. *I don't deserve this kindness. I've ignored them all my life. I could have tried to find Patrick when I was younger, but I was too busy working.*

So, how many times have people ignored me and yet as soon as they cry out for help, I am right there, willing and able to give assistance. This time David didn't move except to scan the room with his eyes just to make sure that there was no one physically in his room.

I've got a lot of work to do here to make up for my past mistakes.

David, you have this all wrong, they extended grace simply because they love you.

How can they love me? They don't know me. I could be a mass murder for all they know.

Do you think they went into this without asking me about it first? They have known for two years that I wanted them to keep this flat for family.

What if John had been locked up instead of me. I certainly wouldn't trust him.

David, who is in control of this whole situation?

Not me, that is for sure. What did I do to deserve this?

Nothing, that's why it's called grace.

But it's too much, too simple.

Trust me when I say, so many people don't get it. They walk away from it simply because they can't accept that it's freely given.

You can't blame them. We're told all our lives that if it looks like it's too good to be true; it usually is.

This is true, sleep now, you need it to be ready for tomorrow.

Morning arrived with the sun streaming through the window waking David with a start. He stretched, realising that he had slept very well for the first time in a very, very long time. A knock on the door, indicated that he really needed to get up.

'David, you awake?' It was Patrick.

'Yes.'

'Jo has made breakfast for you this morning if you are ready. We have three hours before we are needed back at the station, and we need to get that shopping done soon.'

'I'll be right there' he called through the door, as he started pulling on the clothes that he had arrived in yesterday. He completed dressing and opened the door to find Patrick waiting patiently for him to emerge. 'Good morning, sleep well?'

'Yes, I did. Thank you for all you have done.'

'It's no trouble, as Jo said yesterday, you're family.' He turned and walked through to the kitchen where they were met with the smell of bacon, eggs, and toast. Sitting down, he was about to tuck into the meal when Patrick bowed his head and started to say grace. *Oops, I nearly forgot, I'd better remember in the future.* Once grace was over, they all ate with relish.

'We'd better get going. Those new clothes aren't going to appear by magic. Unless we get to the shops, they are not going to appear at all.'

'We'd better go then.' An hour later, with their purchases made and David's hair tidied up, they headed back home. David slipped into his room and changed into a new outfit. He'd forgotten what good clothes felt like, looking in the mirror, he was pleased with the overall look he now presented. He walked back out into the kitchen, where Patrick and Jo were waiting for him.

'We'd better go, they are expecting us.' When they reached the station, they were met by the officer who had let him go into Patrick's care.

'We've investigated the incident and interviewed the lad. He was keen to press charges until we suggested that we talk to his mother, not his father, and tell her that there were several witnesses to the fact that he had injured himself, trying to set up a homeless guy, then he backed down. He almost pleaded with us to talk to his father. We told him that we knew who his father was, that he was a very busy man, and we wouldn't consider it reasonable to interrupt him at work. It seems the lad is more afraid of his mother than his father. You are free to go.' David looked at Patrick and then back at the officer.

'Are you sure?'

'Very sure, just be thankful that you have found your family and you now have a home.' Patrick and David walked out of the station, crossed the carpark to his car. David looked at Patrick.

'Now what?'

'We go home.'

8

That night at dinner, David again asked the question that he had asked Patrick in the carpark. 'What now?'

'Well, can you tell us how you got to this point. Knowing that might help us work out how to move forward.' Patrick asked.

'I don't rightly know. I started off by giving Ben all the attention that I thought he needed and worked hard so that he would have a good business to step into when the time was right. Ben is a tough negotiator, and he was always going to be a great asset to the business, however, he seemed to lack patience and wanted it faster than I was prepared to give it to him. As he got older, I thought he was taking an interest in the business, which he was, but after telling him to be patient a few times he seemed to become distant. It appears that he was working with other members of the board behind the scenes. I didn't realise that Harry was also losing patience with me and wanted to move the company in a different direction. I'm pretty sure it was he who groomed Ben to take over. He had some brilliant business ideas but wasn't too fussed about how ethical their implementation was. He must have been in Ben's ear about how old fashioned I was for a lot longer than I was aware of.'

'Well, that's how the devil works, slowly, chipping away just a little bit at a time. He can be patient if he knows his prey is an easy target.' Jo remarked.

'I was in shock at that board meeting, I couldn't believe that they had tricked me into to signing over all my shares to Ben. I had talked to Harry about giving him ten percent for his twenty first birthday, but not all of them. When they showed me the paperwork, with my signature on it, I was dumfounded. I must have been distracted by something and not realised what I was signing but in the light of the evidence, there was nothing I could do at the time. Even Beth said that we would get by and let God deal with it. That was all very well, until Beth got sick, then my life really fell apart. Oh, how I miss that woman.' David said, his voice catching in his throat.

Patrick squeezed David's shoulder. 'To some extent Beth was right, we will just have to pray for Ben and his family for now, but in the meantime, you need to find some work, so you have some way of supporting yourself. You have a home here, but you do need to be able to buy clothes and food. So, let me talk to a couple of people who I know are looking for workers, and see what happens.'

'Sounds good to me, I want to pay my way, but Ben or Harry made sure I couldn't get a job after they disposed of me. No matter where I went, they wouldn't employ me. It was a miracle that Beth was offered a job a couple of months before Harry and Ben pulled their stunt. Without that job we wouldn't have been able to pay the rent, which was another thing they insisted we do because the company owned the house, and I was no longer part of the company. The fact that we were able to keep it up to date is the only reason that they couldn't put us both out on the street and I made damn sure that the house and garden was kept in good order so they wouldn't have any excuse to evict us. I expected to be put on the street when Beth got sick, I wasn't able to pay the rent after that, but at least they waited until she died before they turned me out, they did that while I was at her funeral. I came home to find the locks changed and my stuff on the front lawn.'

'Okay…. It's been a long time now, and these guys are mates of mine. It will only be manual work but at least it will be something. Are you up for that?' Patrick said.

'If I keep my head down and just do my job, hopefully Ben won't even know that I'm still around. I'm too old to be trying to take the company back off him anyway. I just want him to see me as a father, not a competitor, or the enemy, which is what it seems to be at present.'

'I'll make those calls.' Patrick said as he left the table.

****

After working for a few weeks as a labourer for Terry Jackson, David was starting to feel much better. His strength was coming back, mind you, those first few weeks had proved tiring, and his muscles had

41

complained bitterly every night when he climbed into bed. He had a reason to get up in the morning now and with the money he earned, he had paid Patrick and Jo for the clothes that they had purchased and was paying board. Jo was happy to pack a lunch for him and cook his evening meal. He had breakfast on his own but was grateful for the company at night. Jo was a good listener, and he could depend on her to give a different viewpoint to some of the things that were bothering him. He might be ten years older than these people, but right now, he felt as if he was a teenager just learning the ropes again.

****

9

'Do I have to, mum.' John protested.

'Yes, you do. Your grandfather is ill, and you are going to come with me to visit him. I still wish that you would find something sensible to do with your life. You're seventeen now, it's time for you to start thinking about your future. If you don't start to make some real money of your own soon, how do you expect to be able to provide the things that a wife or family will want? Do you think the things that we have given you came out of thin air? Your grandfather worked very hard to make sure that your father was in a position to provide for me and you. So, you are going to visit and for once you are going to appear to be happy to be there.'

'Oh, mum.. I make real money at the store after school.'

'Don't "Oh mum" me. Enough! That sort of money isn't going to allow you to buy a house or even a car of your own. You are going and I'll not hear any more complaints.'

John sulked in the back seat of the car all the way over to his grandfather's home. His mother had been constantly nagging him to make something of his life lately. He wasn't interested in any one particular girl at present, he was too busy having a good time playing around with as many girls as he could. Why his mother was suddenly concerned about his future was beyond him. It wasn't as if his father was going to step down from his place in the business any time soon. He had never shown any interest in John learning the ropes. What would he do? He still had another year at school to complete anyway, so what was her hurry?

They pulled up in the driveway of his grandparent's home and he slowly got out of the car. His grandmother opened the door as if she had been waiting for them to arrive.

They followed her into the living room, where his grandfather was sitting in a recliner rugged up against the cold, even though the room felt really hot.

Hello son, how are you doing.' His grandfather's voice sounded feeble.

'I'm okay, how about you?'

'Well, I've been better, but I'm not going to let this thing lick me.'

John looked at his mother, and she smiled sadly. 'Oh, course you are dad, you're the toughest guy I know. I'm going to go and help mum with the coffees. I'll be right back.'

As his mother left the room, his grandfather returned his attention to John.

'So, lad, what are you planning to do after school?'

'Oh, not you too Grandpa! Mum's been at me for weeks now. I have no idea what I want to do after I finish school.'

'John, you need to get ready to take over from your father'.

'How? He's in no hurry to step down. I'll be as old as you when that happens.'

'Mate, there's more than one way to skin a cat, haven't you heard. I made sure that your father stepped into the top job long before you were born, and I can help you do the same.'

'How?'

'I want you to come here tomorrow and meet a pal of mine. He is working alongside your father. He is willing to teach you all about the business and how to acquire the necessary votes to take over as soon as you turn twenty-one. It will mean that for the next four years you will have to work hard, learn fast, and keep quiet about these visits.'

'But Grandpa, why would you want to do this to my dad?'

'It appears that your father has been seeing another woman at the office and it's time for him to go. The fact that I need to wait four years to make it happen is okay with me, it will actually give me a reason to beat this thing, because I want to see his face when you step into his shoes.

He thinks that I'm too ill to do anything, well I'm going to show him. You don't cross Harry Burns, or upset his daughter, and get away with it. NEVER!'

John sat down on the couch as if he had been punched. *Apparently, I'd be better off to not upset either of them as well,* he thought, the anger in his grandfather's voice frightened him. He might only be seventeen, and working at the grocery store after school for the last couple of years had taught him a few things about dealing with people, however, he could see no other recourse but to go along with his grandfather's plan. It even occurred to him that his mother might have had more to do with this than she was letting on.

'Okay, Grandpa. I'll see you tomorrow then.' John was relieved to see that his mother had walked back into the room at that point, but he got the impression that she had been waiting just outside the door until her father had made his speech.

John took his coffee cup from the tray that his mother was holding. He drank it slowly and for the first time in his life, he started to take notice of what was going on around him, really take notice, but he was also very careful not to let on to the others in the room that he was very interested in their interactions. He watched his mother, fuss over her father. She didn't make that sort of fuss over his dad. He'd only ever heard her complain to him from the minute he walked in the door, or totally ignore him, depending on what mood she was in. John could understand, even with his limited experience, why his father might have been seeing someone else. How his mother and grandfather had found out, if it was true of course, was of concern. If he was to play this game properly, and it was a very serious game, he was well aware that, he needed to make sure that they didn't find out when he did something they didn't agree with.

John remained thoughtful all the way home. *Who knew that two people could hate someone that much?* The question that John had now was what did his dad's father do to make his grandfather hate him enough to dispose of him? He now realised that the man was capable of a powerful amount of hate, so it occurred to John that maybe it might have been a very small thing, and for the first time in his life he started to feel sorry for his paternal grandfather, even his father, but he had chosen a course to follow and follow it he must, for the time being at least. Maybe this was not the last "first" he was to experience. Deep down he was hoping, that somewhere along this journey, he would be able to change direction because he certainly wasn't comfortable about where this was taking him.

He thought back to the day that he and Liz had come across his grandfather living on the street. Had it really been him? He was never sure, but the likeness to his father was uncanny. He remembered how they had lied to their father about that encounter the next night at dinner. The police had called at the school that day and questioned him about what had happened. They had threatened to call his mother and he wasn't going to have them do that. He knew that if she found out that they had staged the attack his life would not have been worth living. His mother's punishment methods were long lasting and very unpleasant. After watching her with her father today, he had the feeling that those two were very much alike.

Well, he'd play their game for the moment.

****

David is that you? David could hear excitement in Jo's voice as he entered the front door after work. 'When you are ready, I have something to show you.'

When he had finished removing the work dust and dirt and changed, he went and found Jo in the kitchen.

'Come out to the sunroom' she said smiling. 'At the Op shop today, someone found a box of photo albums. They were going to throw them out, but curiosity got the better of me and I picked one up and was looking through it, when I saw a familiar face, yours!'

'What! What do you mean?'

'David, I think those photo albums are yours or belonged to your family. Maybe Ben threw them out. Come and have a look and see what you think.'

Sure enough, there in the box was the photo albums that Beth had so carefully put together over the years. She didn't take a lot of photos but the ones she did take she made sure to put into albums, carefully. There were photos of their wedding day, Ben as a baby, his school photos, and one at his twenty-first birthday party. Oh, he had been so proud that night. His son had grown into a man, and he looked every bit the executive. He'd planned to have Ben voted onto the board at the meeting on Monday morning. Little did he realise, that at that same meeting, the board would vote him out of the company altogether, installing Ben as Chairman, because apparently, he had signed all his shares over to Ben. David shook his head, even after all this time, he could never figure out how they had pulled it off legally, well, it probably wasn't legal, but he had been in shock, and it was too painful to look at too deeply. David had gone from proud to horrified in ten minutes. He had been given two hours to clear his office. David knew, from what Patrick had been able to find out, that Ben's twins would be turning twenty-one in a few months. *I wonder how Ben will feel at their party?*

'David are you okay?'

'Yeah sure, I just can't believe that these have turned up after all this time. Do you know how they came to be at the store?'

'Only that the people were cleaning out their roof space to add some extensions and found them up there.'

'You don't know what address?'

'No.'

'I can't imagine Beth putting them there, she wasn't well enough to do anything for months before she died. Unless she got someone else to put them there in the early stages of her illness. Now that I think about it, I hadn't seen these for months before she died.'

47

Maybe she realized that Ben would have made sure they were disposed of if they were found in the actual house. Very few people look in roof spaces. I heard the company did a bang up clean out of the house after I was evicted. Well, God has brought them back to me. Is that Patrick coming home? Let's see what he thinks of this?'

'Hello.'

'We're out in the sunroom. I found these photos of David's at the shop today, and we were just having a look through them.'

'Wow.'

'This is Ben at his twenty-first. I was so proud of him. I couldn't believe what happened on the following Monday, just when I was going to have him voted onto the board.'

'Well, we have spent a lot of time praying for him and his family since you have been here, so we will continue, and now we have some photos to help us. He does look a lot like you.'

'Yeah. But his daughter looks like Beth, I thought she had come back to haunt me that day I was arrested. Man, they could be the same person.'

'I never met Beth, this is a really nice way to put a face to a name, even after all these years.' Patrick said thoughtfully as he searched deeper into the box. 'Oh, look, there's a photo in a frame. It's your wedding photo and here's one of Ben on his twenty-first.'

'Please, David, let me clean these up and put them up with our other family photos. That will be a good way to tell our friends that you are family, real family. Oh, does that sound weird?'

'Yes, a bit, but good, weird,' David laughed. 'The twins will be twenty-one soon. I would love to have been part of that, but God knows what is happening to them and Ben. I have to trust him on this but it's not easy.'

'Hang in there, mate, as you said, God is in control.'

10

It was a Friday night, and his mother had organised a lavish party for their twenty-first birthday. His grandfather had indicated that he would be replacing his father as chairman of the business. A vote to this effect would be taken at a meeting of the Board of Directors sometime soon. His grandfather had only said that he had a very special gift for him, and he was going to give it to him at the party that night. John had been a little mystified by the comment but let it go after all this was a joint party, for both him and his twin sister, Liz. Surely his grandfather wouldn't ignore her on her special night. The excitement of the party made it easy for him to push any concerns he might have had to the back of his mind.

****

Tonight, was the twins' twenty-first birthday party. Where had the time gone? They were adults now, well and truly. Ben walked into the foyer of their home, where the three of them were waiting for him. The twins were standing together, Liz dressed in a sapphire blue dress that was surprisingly modest but made her look stunning. He smiled at her and noticed that John was looking very mature in his tux. As he stepped forward, he noticed that Gloria was wearing the same dress that she had worn to the party on the night that he had got her drunk and which they credited with the conceiving of the twins.

'How come you're wearing that dress again?' he asked surprised.

'So, you remember this dress then?'

'Yes?'

'Yes, Ben, it's the dress I wore the night you got me pregnant. It seemed like a good time to wear it again, on their twenty-first birthday.'

'Well, it looks as good on you now as it did then' Ben said, ignoring the obvious sarcasm in her voice. *You have to give it to Gloria; she could hold a grudge for a long time.*

****

Boy, thought John, *I wonder what that's about?* He glanced at Liz and noticed that she also had a puzzled look on her face.

'Shall we go?' John you can drive tonight.' His father handed him the keys and moved towards the door, and they all followed him out to the car.

****

When the family arrived at the party, Ben and Gloria reached the double doors, and in a rare unspoken act of working together, they opened a door each and stepped aside to allow the twins to enter first. It was their night after all, and they needed to take centre stage. Once the applause died down, Ben and Gloria moved around the room separately, Gloria headed towards her parents, while Ben drifted towards some of the board of directors, but they didn't seem that inclined to engage in conversation with him. A strange feeling came over him as he made his way to the bar and the buffet table. *I wonder what dad would make of this.* The thought arrived out of the blue. He hadn't thought about his father in a long time.

****

John noticed that his grandfather was starting to look tired, if he wanted to make a special announcement tonight, it had better be soon or he will be falling asleep in that wheelchair. As that thought crossed his mind, his mother moved the wheelchair towards the microphone. *This is it,* he thought. The band stopped playing.

****

Ben was watching his father-in-law; he was very thin, and his skin had a grey look about it. He had been ill for four years now and it had amazed his doctors that he had lasted this long. He was starting to look like he was ready to collapse, and he was about to suggest that it might be time for him to call it a night when Gloria helped him move to the microphone.

50

'Good evening, everyone. It's been a wonderful evening I'm sure you will all agree.' Harry's voice was surprisingly strong for a man who was so ill. 'It's such a special occasion when one's grandchildren reach the age of twenty-one. I've watched them grow since they were very little and now, they are fully fledged adults. Yes, I know that eighteen is now considered the age of adulthood but I'm a very old-fashioned man. So, it would seem that tonight is the right time to make a very special announcement. John, can you please come up here and stand beside me.' John looked at his father and moved forward, his legs felt as if they were made of lead as his grandfather continued. 'Earlier today, the board of Bannister Industries met and voted John, my grandson, as their new chairman. He will take over the position on Monday.' There was a smattering of applause. John looked around at the gathering and noticed that the only people applauding were members of the board, everyone else just looked stunned; his grandfather continued by addressing his father directly.

'Your father wouldn't listen to me and so I had you take his place. You hurt my daughter by taking a mistress, and so your son takes your place. He knows his place and will do me proud.'

'Damn you, Harry, she hurt me more.' Ben shot back at his father-in-law. 'Enjoy your victory because I suspect it won't be for long.' Ben turned and walked out of the building.

Ben walked down the street, on autopilot, heading towards home. His gut hurt as if he had been physically hit with a sledgehammer. The look of satisfaction on both Harry and Gloria's faces burnt into his brain. I knew she could hold a grudge, but boy, that's beyond belief. *Well, now I know how dad felt when it happened to him*, Ben thought, remembering the shocked look on his father's face. But that had been in the board room not at a public function. What made Ben even angrier was the fact that those two had managed to ruin Liz and John's birthday party. The man got worse as he got older, and so did his own wife, it would seem. How dare they do that, particularly to Liz. John, well he was going to go to work on Monday in his place, but Liz got nothing except a ruined party.

If there was anything to give him satisfaction it was the fact that the great announcement seemed to fall flat, there wasn't the big acclamation that he knew Harry would have expected. *SERVES HIM RIGHT!* Ben had looked at John when Harry had made his pointed remarks to him directly, and he knew by the look on his son's face, that he wasn't happy, and he hadn't expected what his grandfather had said. The man was ill, but that didn't excuse his behaviour tonight and Ben felt no regrets for telling him to enjoy his victory while he could.

He arrived home and found the spare key. He let himself in, walked around the dark house, poured a drink, and sat down at the table. He really should try and find out if his father was still alive and say sorry.

****

Most people decided that it was time to go home, the announcement by Harry Burns had left a sour note on the proceedings and so they quietly gathered their things and left one by one. John noticed that his grandfather suddenly looked very tired. His moment of triumph had fallen well below his expectations.

'Grandpa, I think it might be time you went home and got some rest.'

'Yes, I think you might be right. Gloria, will you take us home please we used a taxi to get here, and I suggest that you stay at our place tonight. I don't think Ben is going to be happy to see you when he gets home.'

John handed his mother the keys which were in his pocket and helped his grandparents out to their family car.

'How will you get home? Gloria asked, turning to John

'We'll walk, we will be okay, don't worry.'

Liz and John stood side by side and watched their mother driving off down the road.

'Wow, I didn't see that coming, it was a bit rough on dad' Liz said

'I know, I knew it was going to happen, but not like that.'

'You knew they were going to do that' Liz voice rose in shock.

'Yeah, sort of. I didn't know about him shaming him over the mistress thing though. I knew he thought something was going on but that wasn't fair, to dad or us. Mum has never treated him nicely, not that justifies him having a bit on the side, but I can understand him wanting someone to just be nice to him. John paused. 'Let's go home.'

'Shouldn't we try and find dad?'

'Do you think he is going to want to see me right now? Besides my car is at the house. No, let's go home, hopefully he will turn up before morning. He may have walked straight home. If he hasn't turned up by morning, then we can report him missing. It's not that far, and besides, I could use a very strong cup of coffee about now.'

The house was in darkness as they walked up the footpath. There was no indication that their father was home. John opened the door and let Liz enter first. She turned on the hall light and made her way to the kitchen. When she turned that light on, their father was sitting at the table with a drink in his hand staring into space.

***

Ben wasn't sure how long he had been sitting there when the light flicked on, and Liz was standing in the doorway.

'Dad.. You, okay?' Liz asked, concern showing in her voice.

'Yeah. I will be. I'm sorry that your night was ruined like that. Where's John?'

'Right here.' John's voice was quiet.

'You might have at least given me a heads-up mate. I knew those two were cooking something up, but nothing like that.'

'I'm sorry dad. I had no idea he was going to go that far, and I wasn't told when the board meeting was going to be held, I thought it might have been Monday. I don't agree with what is happening, you know; I just didn't have the energy to fight both of them on this. I'll see what I can do later but right now I'm just playing along.'

'Mate, it's alright. I had time to think on the way home and now I understand how my father felt when he was turfed out. To my shame, I was rougher on my father than that was on me tonight. I took on Harry's and your mother's hatred and poured it all over my father and mother, which is why he ended up homeless. The only thing I wouldn't let Harry do, was turn them out of their home while mum was alive. After that, Harry made sure my father ended up on the streets. Like you, I didn't have the backbone to fight him and your mother either.'

'How does a man develop that much hate?'

'I don't know. There will be something in his childhood no doubt that triggered it, I guess. Look I know you have to go to work on Monday, but over the weekend I would like to try and find my father. No chance you can help, I suppose.'

'I will.' Liz volunteered, 'John had better stay close to home over the weekend. Just in case grandpa tries to check up on him. How did he find out you had a mistress anyway?'

'I didn't, but I can understand why he may have thought I did. I had the spare office made into a sitter and I would sleep there some nights when your mother was in a particularly bad mood. Barry Stone came into my office one morning and saw the pull-out bed unmade. I'd had a particularly bad night and it could've look like two people had been sleeping in it; he must have put two and two together and came up with six instead of four. He never said anything to me, but it seems he had an almighty good whinge to your grandfather. Mind you, there were times when I was tempted, and that was part of the intention when I had the office revamped, but when it actually came down to it, I just couldn't do it. I'd invite people in there for a drink and we'd talk for hours but it was always couples or groups. You have to believe me.'

'It's okay dad, we watched mum for years and we have seen how other wives are treated, we're not totally clueless. Mum was a handful. What was the thing about the dress tonight? That was weird.' Liz asked.

'You're not going to like this; your mother was never keen on having kids. Your grandparents wanted us to have some, and I wanted her to give me something that I couldn't give myself. A baby was the only thing that fitted the bill. So, the night she wore that dress to the party, I pretended to have a headache and she was very drunk, so when we got home, I was able to subdue her pretty easily. She wasn't happy when she found out she was pregnant, and even less happy when you turned out to be twins, but she does love you and so do I, even if I haven't been the best father in the world. Anyway, we'd better get some sleep, I want to see if I can find my father tomorrow, if he's even still alive. Thank you for helping me, Liz. I don't deserve it.'

'You're my father. We wouldn't be here without you and to be honest, we owe your father an apology too. We weren't honest with you all those years ago when we told you about seeing him on the street.'

'I think we have had enough confessions for one night, let's get to bed,' John cut in, 'and we will continue to work the rest out in the morning.' His father looked tired, but John wasn't surprised, he'd had the stuffing punched out him, but hopefully some sleep would help him feel a little better in the morning. John wasn't sure if he'd be able to sleep well either, but he was too tired to stand up any longer.

11

Ben woke as the phone beside his bed rang. The clock told him that it was only four in the morning.

'Hello', his voice was still groggy with sleep.

'Ben, Dad's been taken to hospital, he's had a stroke and they don't expect him to live very long. The doctors told me to call his family. Can you bring the kids?' Gloria's voice was shrill with panic.

'We'll be right there.' He looked at the doorway to see the twins standing there looking confused.

'What's happened?' Liz asked.

'It appears your grandfather has had a stroke and we need to get to the hospital. Get dressed and I'll make some coffee to drink on the way.

'You're dressed?' John exclaimed.

'Yeah, I couldn't be bothered changing, I just laid down and went to sleep.

The twins moved and he made his way to the kitchen. With the coffee made in travel mugs, he handed them to his kids as they made their way to John's car.

God, I didn't expect this. Now what? The words were thrown out from his brain silently into space. He hadn't even thought about, let alone spoken to, God since he was a child and his mother had made him say his prayers every night.

Just follow my lead!

'What did you say?' Ben looked at John concentrating on the road.

'Nothing, I didn't say a thing.' He replied, Ben shook his head, was the stress too much, was he going mad?

They drove the rest of the way in silence and were quietly shown to the hospital room, where Gloria and her mother sat beside Harry's bed. His body appeared to be lifeless, *we're too late*, he thought.

Gloria's mother lent forward, touching Harry on the arm, 'Harry, the twins and Ben are here.' His eyes flickered open, he turned his head and looked at them. Ben saw real fear in those eyes, and he tried to say something but all that would come out was moans and groans. A nurse checked Harry's vital signs, shook her head slightly and left the room. It was then that Ben noticed that there were three more chairs available and so he pulled one closer and sat down.

Now what? Ben looked around the room. It was cold and stark, painted white with a metal cabinet next to him.

Open the drawer. The instruction, Ben realised, was from a voice in his head, similar to what he had heard in the car on the way over.

Ben opened the drawer and lying there on its own was a Bible. *Goodness, I haven't opened one of these since I was a kid,* he thought as he took it out and turned it over in his hand.

Open it, again that voice was insistent.

Where?

Just open it

Okay, Ben opened it and it fell open at Psalm 23.

Read aloud.

What?

Read aloud, Harry needs to hear this before he runs out of time.

Okay……..

'The Lord is my shepherd'…. Ben looked at the others in the room, no one seemed to object, so he kept reading. 'I shall not want….'

As he finished that Psalm the voice in his head said, keep going. So, he kept reading. The more he read, the calmer Harry seemed to get. About half-way through Psalm 34, Harry closed his eyes. Ben nearly stopped reading but decided to carry on until he had finished that particular Psalm.

After he stopped, Harry opened his eyes again. He looked at Ben, then Gloria, his wife, and the twins. Ben saw his grip on his wife's hand tighten. Everyone could see that he was trying to say something; then suddenly, the words, 'I'm sorry, forgive me, Jesus, can you all forgive me the hate I made?' came out as clear as anything. Gloria cried 'but you didn't hate me'

'No, but I made you hate Ben. Find God's love, all of you.' The effort seemed to drain him of everything he had, and he closed his eyes, smiled, and took his last breath. His wife bent down and placed her forehead on the bed. Gloria cried, Liz went over and wrapped her arms around her mother, Ben reached out and held John's hand. The atmosphere was strange. A couple of minutes later the nurse came in, checked him for a pulse and said, 'I'm sorry, but he's gone now. I'll give you all another couple of minutes and then we'll have to take him down to the morgue.'

Ben waited for what felt like a long time, but eventually he spoke, 'Come on, I think it's time we had breakfast.'

'How can you think of food at a time like this' Gloria spat at him.

'Mum, come on, you look like you're going to pass out any minute.' Liz said. 'Come on, this is not the time to snap at anyone.'

Ben placed the chairs against the wall, opened the door and let the rest of the family exit the room in front of him without saying a word. As he passed the Nurses Station, he handed the nurse his phone number. If there is anything that needs to be done, can you ring me on this number please. I don't think my wife, or her mother are capable of doing much right now.' The nurse nodded and he walked away, catching up with the rest of the family at the elevator.

They entered the shop right across the street from the hospital entrance. It appeared to be open twenty-four hours. Ben guessed that being that close they probably had customers coming in at all hours of the day and night.

'May I take your order,' the waitress spoke in a quietly calm voice.

'Coffee, everyone?' Ben looked around the group, everyone nodded.

'How about I bring you a large pot, mugs, milk and sugar and you can all help yourselves when you are ready.'

'Thank you,' Ben looked at her for the first time and he could see sympathy in her eyes.

'It's okay, we get many grieving families in here.' Ben smiled and she walked away to get their coffee.

'Dad, do you think we could just have some pancakes, I suddenly feel pretty hungry.' Liz asked quietly.

'Yeah, sure, I'll order them when our coffee arrives. That okay with the rest of you?' Again, the nods were all he had to go on.

The food was ordered, and they ate in silence. They even managed to get through another pot of coffee but eventually he knew that it was time for them to move.

'Mum,' he addressed his mother-in-law, 'do you want to go home or come back to our place for a couple of days?'

'Could I stay at your place, just until I figure out what I'm meant to do, that house is so big, too big for one person.'

'No problem, Liz, you take your grandmother back to her place so she can collect some things, Gloria you go with Liz and help your mother. John and I will go to the office and start making some phone calls to the board members. We'll see you at home when we are finished.'

'Dad, I'm not going to take up that position, not now.'

'Son, they voted you in, it's part of your job. The rest of this mess can be sorted out later. We'll split the list, you can do half and I'll ring the other half.

****'

Ben and John arrived home not long after the women, there was a heavy atmosphere around the house, no one wanted to do anything so mostly they sat in silence.

Later in the afternoon, Liz found her father in the lounge.

'Dad, you know what we talked about last night, … About finding your father, do you still want to do that.'

'Yeah, but let's leave it until tomorrow, hey'

'Yeah, sure.'

'Gloria looked at her daughter and then her husband, 'You're going to find your father?'

'Yeah, I realised last night how badly I treated him, and I need to find him and say I'm sorry. If he is still alive, that is.' It was not an accident that he had said I instead of we, he wasn't prepared to fight with her over the part that she and her father had played in the sordid affair.

****

Where would you like to start to look for Pop?' Liz asked her father the next morning at breakfast.

'I have no idea,'

'Why not start at the Police station at Lillydale, they would know if he was locked up after that stunt we pulled six years ago.' John interjected.

'That sounds like a good place to start. John you'd better stay here just in case the women need something or someone rings, I think you will be the best person to answer any questions people might have.' Ben looked

60

at his son's disappointed face. 'We are just trying to find out if he's alive at this point, you will get to see him later, hopefully.'

'Okay, give me half an hour and we'll go.' Liz said as she moved away from the table.

****

Once they had hit the open road between the two towns, Ben who was driving, finally felt that it was time to ask the question that had been bothering him since breakfast.

'What was the stunt that you guys pulled that John mentioned this morning.?'

'Oh, that... John made out that pop had attacked him. That's why the Police took him away. In fact, John gave himself some small stab wounds after he made me attack him.'

'So, that's what you meant last night when you said that you owed him an apology. I had a feeling at the time that there was more to the story than what I was being told. It was that night that I decided that you both needed to start learning how live in the real world.'

'Yeah, in our defence we were only silly, spoilt teenagers at the time.'

'Yeah, I know. I'm surprised at how grown up you both are, considering the way we treated you. Let's hope that someone was able to help him.'

'The best thing you did for us was make us get jobs of our own. That's where we saw how different things were in the real world.'

'John surprised me though, I'd have thought that with all the time he was spending with his grandfather that he would have been more like him. He certainly wasn't last night.'

Grandpa made one big mistake. He had Jack Buchannan mentor him and he was able to help him see that there was a better way to live than the way Grandpa was.'

'Wow, you knew about this?'

'Not all of it, no, but most of it. Dad, we are twins, when we're not fighting, we are best mates who talk, and bounce things off each other. We have always been good mates generally, particularly now that we are older. He was only appearing to go along with them, Grandpa, and Mum, but I know that he is hoping to get you back in the chairman's seat sooner rather than later, it will be easier now that Grandpa isn't calling the shots.'

'Yes, but he still has to deal with his mother.'

'We know, but again, Grandpa isn't calling the shots anymore. Mum might be different now that he is gone.'

'Maybe,…. besides, I don't deserve to be there either. Your grandfather, if he is still alive, should still be in that chair.'

'Well, here we are, this is it,' Liz said, closing down the conversation as they pulled up outside the Police Station.

Ben and Liz walked up to the counter.

'Can I help you.' The Police officer looked up. 'Oh, my, you look exactly like your grandmother, Liz Bannister, isn't it?'

'Yeah, how did you know, this is my dad..'

'Ben Bannister. You haven't changed much either.'

'Do I know you.' Ben asked suspiciously.

'No, but I know your father. David Bannister is my cousin and has been living with us for several years. Now, what may I do for you.'

'Well, the reason we are here is….. to try and find my father.'

'Hum, can I ask why you might want to do that after all this time?'

'I've come to realise that I treated him very badly all those years ago and I would like to ask him to forgive me, even if he doesn't want to have anything to do with me after that.' Ben said

'I also need to apologise to him for the way we treated him six years ago.' Liz added.

'And John?'

'He's sorry too, but at the moment he is holding the fort at home. Our other grandfather died yesterday in the early hours of the morning.'

'Oh, I see. I'm sorry about your grandfather. I'll need to ring my wife, but I finish my shift soon, so you can follow me home in about fifteen minutes if you like.'

'That would be great. I don't know if he will be happy to see me after all this time, but I have to try and say I'm sorry.'

'Ben, your father,….. we all, ….. have been praying for you for a long time. Tread gently, but I'm sure that he will at least listen to what you have to say. There's a seat outside, enjoy the sun for the next few minutes and I'll come and get you when I'm ready to leave.'

****

With his father and Liz away from the house, John felt at a bit of a loose end. He wandered into the lounge room to see his mother, red eyed and quietly crying. This surprised him, because usually when his mother cried, she made a major performance out of it, so he quickly concluded that these tears were very real, which made him feel sorry for her. It seemed that even really bad people are loved by their children and Harry had doted on his mother, even if it was for his own selfish reasons.

'Mum?'

'Oh, I'm sorry John.'

'Can I get you a cup of tea or coffee?'

'Tea would be nice, thank you'

John looked at his mother and went to make her tea. He returned and passed it to her, 'Where's Grandma?'

'Having a lie down'

'Are you okay?'

'Yeah, just going over yesterday morning at the hospital.'

'Yeah, that was weird. What did Grandpa mean when he said he made you hate dad?'

'That's mostly what I've been thinking about. I really did love your father when I first met him. It was love at first sight. I'm just starting to realise that dad must have seen it and pushed us together for his own selfish purposes. He was looking for a way to get rid of your pop and he used us to make it happen.'

'So, why?'

'Oh, I don't know. The only person who knows that now isn't here to explain. Maybe it was something he said, or a decision that he made without consulting him. I have no idea, John, I really don't.'

'But how did he make you hate dad?'

'Oh, he was clever. He would make snide remarks about Ben not giving me some little thing or his daughter not living it up in a house that displayed our position in the company, that sort of thing, and I always wanted him to be pleased with me, which he never was of course, and so I'd take it out on your father. If I told dad that Ben wasn't going to give me something then he would just tell me to behave badly, or sweetly, whatever it took to get what I wanted, which now I realise is what he wanted. It's become such a bad habit that I'm not sure I can stop. Oh, John I want to stop! I don't want to live like that anymore.'

'Mum, I think you're telling the wrong person. You've made a choice, now stick to it. When dad comes home you have to make a choice every time you open your mouth, be nice and see what happens.'

'What if I can't!'

'You will have times when you will fall back into your old habits, but one thing Jack taught me, was that it's okay to fall down, but it's not okay to not get up and start again. It doesn't matter how many times you fall, what counts is how many times you get back up.'

Gloria looked at John as if she was seeing him for the first time. 'How did I have a son who was so smart?'

'Thank Jack for most of it, I should think,' he smiled to take the sting out of his words.

****

David heard the phone ringing in the main house. He'd had a couple of bad nights, so for now he was sitting in his living room trying to read his Bible. Ben had been on his mind, disturbing his sleep. He had prayed and prayed but he still felt unsettled. There was a knock on the door to his flat.

'David, it's Jo. Can I come in?'

'Yeah, sure.'

'That was Patrick on the phone. He is bringing Ben and his daughter home when his shift finishes. They turned up at the station looking for you.'

'Really? Ben has been on my mind so much in the last couple of days, I've had trouble sleeping. I wonder what's going on.'

'Well, we're about to find out.'

'Can you come and help me sort out some food? I'm glad I cooked that extra cake yesterday.'

'You always seem to hear the promptings from God, but I hope this kid of mine isn't going to start rubbing salt into my wounds again.'

'David, have some faith, I have a good feeling about this.'

'Well, I hope you are right,' he said, as they walked out to the kitchen together. David's stomach was full of butterflies though. Regardless of how long you have been praying for something, when it actually looks like it's being answered, the nerves give you merry hell, he decided.

Patrick walked into the kitchen, followed by two people.

'Jo, this is Ben Bannister and his daughter Liz.'

'Wow, David wasn't wrong when he said that you look like your grandmother. Welcome, came and sit down, I've made us morning tea.'

Hello Dad,' Ben said nervously, as David stepped forward, stretched out his arm, ready to shake his hand. He was going to at least give this reconciliation a fair crack even if it wasn't what was on the boys' mind. Ben shook his hand. 'Dad, I'm sorry. I acted like a jerk, a very big jerk, and I don't expect you to forgive me, not after all this time but I had to at least tell you that I've realised what I did was wrong. I guess I always knew it was, I just didn't have the courage to admit it until now.'

'Son, I forgave you a long time ago, but it is nice to hear you admit to it. Come on, let's have a cuppa and we can talk.'

Over the next couple of hours, Ben and Liz filled Patrick, Jo, and David in about what had happened, admitting that a lot of it was a result of them not having the courage to stand up to Harry. Ben also told them about the hospital visit and reading the Bible to Harry on his death bed.

'It sounds like he found forgiveness right at the end. If that is the case, and only God knows for sure, you will get to see him again in Heaven.' Patrick said.

'It hardly seems fair. He got to create all this grief while he was alive and on his death bed, he asks God to forgive him, he goes to Heaven, and we are left still having to clean up the destruction he left behind.' Ben's tone was miserable.

'I understand you feeling that way, but that is what grace is, and God is a very gracious and merciful God, it's the undeserved gift that He gives

66

us when we come to Jesus seeking forgiveness. He said, "ask and it will be given". That applies to anyone asking for forgiveness even at the last moment. Harry's lucky he had time, if he had died instantly, he wouldn't have been able to ask. That is why the word of God tells us not to wait, but to come to Jesus while we can. Too many people put it off and sadly not everyone gets a last-minute chance, like Harry did. Also, if you hadn't followed the voice in your head that told you to read the Bible, he still wouldn't have had the opportunity. However, you did, and God will honour that; he will give you the strength, courage, and inspiration that will be necessary to clean up the mess he left behind. All you have to do is ask as well.'

Patrick took a sip of his tea and then continued. 'That fear, that you told us you saw in his eyes when you got to the hospital, it's most likely that he knew he was going to live with the torment for eternity, having spent a lot of time with people during their last moments on earth as part of my policework, it seems to me that a lot of them have definite spiritual clarity once they know they are dying and he would have known that his time on earth was up. Would you honestly want the man to live with that fear forever, even with what he has done?

'No, I guess not.' Ben said thoughtfully.

Besides, when you meet him again, he will be the best version of who he is. No more bullying, he will be a new person and that is something to look forward to, isn't it? I find it very interesting that Christians who won't talk to each other here on earth, will, once they get to Heaven, be on the best of terms.'

'Yes, I hadn't thought about that.' Ben smiled, glancing at his watch. 'My goodness is that the time, we need to get back home, but Dad, I want to see what I can do about restoring your position on the board. Tomorrow they expect John to take over which we will have to allow to happen, but Liz tells me that he isn't happy about the way it was done, unlike me.' Ben dropped his face into his hands, rubbed his eyes and forehead before he went on. 'Please give us some time to see how the board reacts to the death of Harry and formulate a plan but I promise you I want to make things right.'

'Son, I've waited this long, a few more months won't make any difference. I'm not sure that I want to return to the board anyway. I have a job as a labourer now and I'm finding that I get along well with the men and it's helping me to keep fit. You do what you have to do and don't be a stranger. You need to take your time and sort out things at home as well. Just let me know if there is anything I can do to help, and I will continue to pray for all of you.'

****

Ben passed the keys to Liz, 'You drive home please.'

'Sure, you, okay?'

'Yeah, just a lot of thinking to do and I may not be able to concentrate properly.'

'Fair enough' she started the car and waited for her father to put his seatbelt on.

Ben was grateful that Liz didn't press him for his thoughts as they drove home.

Prayer must be a powerful thing, Ben thought, *if John had treated me the way I treated dad, I would have been tempted to literally put my hands around his throat and yet, dad extended his hand in friendship. But he's right I need to sort out stuff at home before I can fix this mess. There will be no point trying to bring dad back into the business if Gloria is going to continue to cause trouble the way her father did. I wonder what sort of mood she is going to be in when we get home. I didn't expect to be away this long. Oh God, if you can hear me, please help me put things right with my family.*

Liz parked the car, Ben got out and walked inside, bracing himself for a barrage of words. There was silence! He looked at Liz, she looked at him and frowned.

'Hello?' Ben asked tentatively.

'Oh, you're back, did you find out anything?' Gloria's voice was even and polite.

'Well, yes, he's still alive and living in a granny flat attached to his cousin's house.'

'I didn't know he had any family.'

'I didn't either. He never talked about his childhood, I guess it wasn't something he wanted to discuss.'

'How is he?'

'Very well and pretty fit actually.'

'Is he upset with you?'

'Would you believe me if I told you that he has been praying for us a lot over the last six years and he shook my hand straight up.'

'Actually, somehow, I'm not surprised. I didn't have a lot to do with him, of course, Dad didn't encourage it, but he did seem like a really nice guy.'

'I'll leave you guys to talk', Liz said, 'I'm going to find John and fill him in.' Ben waited until his daughter had left the room and then turned to face Gloria.

'Gloria, can we talk? I mean really talk. I'd like to go for a walk somewhere away from the house and see where we're at.' Ben watched Gloria, *was he pushing this too fast, would talking make things better or worse.*

'Sure, it's a nice afternoon, I'll get my coat.'

They walked along the road until they came to a park area beside the river that ran through their town. There were plenty of tables, seats, and benches for people to sit and watch the wild ducks swim around in the water. They picked a bench and sat down. Ben knew why they had picked this one without having to say anything. This was where they used to sit when they were courting. Sure, it hadn't been for long, but this had been their favourite spot back then. Maybe Gloria also

69

remembered those days when life seemed full of promise, was it a sign that their future was also going to be better. He hoped with all his heart that it was possible.

'Ben, I'm sorry. I've done a lot of thinking while you were away today, and I've realised that I've been a selfish, nasty piece of work over the years. I could cop out and blame dad, but in truth I didn't have to bow to his pressure, I could have made the choice to be nice even while he was telling me to go and get what I wanted any way I could. I don't blame you for having a mistress, your home life wasn't what it shouldn't have been.'

'Gloria, I never had a mistress, never.'

'But dad said you were caught red handed.'

'You do realise that sometimes he embellished the truth, don't you?'

'Yeah, I know, I just ignored it but ...'

'I had a pull-out sofa bed put in the spare office next to mine. When I didn't want to fight with you, I would sleep there instead of going home. One morning Barry walked into my office before I had made the bed up and shut the adjoining door. He must have passed Trudy, who had also had a rough night with her kids and was looking tired, on his way in and I'm assuming that he put two and two together and came up with a cheating husband. He never said anything to me but I'm guessing that he reported it to your father, it's the only thing I can think of that would have given him such an idea. Yes, I admit that when I had that room converted, the thought of having a good time with someone else crossed my mind, but when it came down to it, I loved you and I couldn't do it. Yes, sometimes I would have friends in there for a meal, but they were always couples, never a single woman, or man for that matter, and we would talk, laugh, and have a few drinks. That's it, honestly.'

Gloria turned and looked at him steadily. He could tell that she was trying to work out if he was really telling her the truth, he held her gaze.

70

Finally, she smiled. *My goodness, that smile, I haven't seen that in a long time, and it still lights up my world.*

'Can you forgive me?'

'Yes, of course. You weren't the only one who bowed down to Harry and did his bidding.'

'Ben, you do realise that being mean and nasty has become such a bad habit for me, that I'm likely to relapse often, even though I promise to try and be the wife that I should be. John was telling me earlier that it wasn't the falling down that was the issue but not getting up, that was the real problem.'

'My goodness, John is full of surprises. Liz says that your father made a mistake in getting Jack to mentor him, because he was able to show John how to live in a better manner than your father.'

'John said much the same thing,' Gloria smiled, 'I'm so proud of him, Ben, even if we can't take a lot of credit for his proper upbringing. When mum heard that Jack was an option, she was furious. Dad decided that he was the only person for the job. We've made a real mess of all our lives, haven't we?'

The past is the past and it just has to be dealt with now, so we can move on and make a better life for all of us. After all, we are all adults now, it's time to grow up, I guess.'

They sat and talked for a long time, suddenly there was a loud rumble from his stomach at the same time as a similar noise came from Gloria. They looked at each other and smiled.

'I think it's time we went home and got something to eat' Gloria said.

'Gloria, before we go, I want to ask you something. After we get the funeral and some of the business stuff sorted, I would like to take you out for a proper romantic meal, to sort of mark our new start. Do you think you would be up to that?'

Gloria frowned, *oh dear I've got something wrong here,* thought Ben.

'Gloria, talk to me, please! If we are going to start over, we need to talk to each other, and not assume that we should understand things. I know we have been married a long time, but we have been on a miserable detour and now that we are back on a good road, let's make sure we stay on it.'

'Okay, the date. I like the romantic idea, but a dinner will usually include wine, right?'

'Well, it doesn't have to.'

'You see, Ben, it's like this, you do realise that every time we have made love in the last twenty-two years, I have always been under the influence. I don't want to do that anymore. I want to try and do this stone-cold sober. I'll probably mess it up, but I want to try. Besides, dinner at a restaurant, that's not really my idea of a romantic date.'

'Okay, what would you like to do instead?'

'How about we buy fish and chips and have our date right here. I know the evenings are getting cooler but if we dress warmly, we should be okay. I'll wear my red dress again if it helps to make things more romantic for you.' She was giggling as she said it.

'Oh, no you won't. If you want to wear red, that's fine, you look beautiful in that colour, but please will you go out and buy a new outfit. Just like you, I don't want our new start to be clouded with difficult memories from our old life.'

'Ben, you are a wonderful husband, you know that.' She reached over and kissed him, it wasn't a polite husband and wife peck, it was a proper "I love you" kiss. His heart skipped a beat.

Dinner that night was so relaxed that it felt strange. Gloria's mother looked startled to start with and ate her whole meal without saying a word.

'Mum, are you okay?'

'Yeah, but I have been thinking. I wonder if you two would mind if Liz and John came and stayed with me for a few weeks. Just until I decide what to do with the house.'

Ben looked at each of his kids, *would this be a good idea. Would she also try to turn them against him?*

'John, Liz, is this something that you would be willing to do?'

'Yeah, we'll be happy to do that, but there would be one condition, we all spend the weekends here and that way when you invite Pop over, we all get to spend time with him.'

'I'll make sure that you have some spare meals to take home with you. That way mum won't have to worry about cooking for you. I know how much food John can put away; she'll never keep up.' Gloria said with a smile.

'How about you all wait until after the funeral though, we will have to start getting those arrangements underway tomorrow.' Ben said, part of him wanted Gloria and the house all to himself, but he was also nervous about how that would work out. *Goodness, I'm a grown man, you'd think I would be past being nervous to be alone with my wife, but it's been such a long time since we have done things right, she's probably just as jumpy.* Another part of him was worried about what his mother-in-law might be up to, you don't live with a man like Harry for as long as she did without some of his mannerisms rubbing off on you.

Later that night, he was coming back into the lounge room with a tray of hot drinks, when he heard Gloria talking to her mum, he stopped and waited outside the door and listened.

'Mum, why do you really want the kids to move into the house with you? Surely you're not that worried about being in that house all by yourself?'

'Oh, come on Gloria, I saw the way you and Ben were looking at each other at dinner. I always knew that you were really in love with the man. It was your father who decided that it was going to just be a good business match and nothing else. He never did have a romantic notion

73

in that business head of his. He never had a clue that you and Ben were head over heels for each other. However, if you guys are going to start over again, now that he cannot interfere, and that's certainly what it looked like at dinner, you don't need me and the kids getting in the way. You need to have the house all to yourselves especially at night. That way you can make as much racket as you like.'

Ben walked into the room, just in time to see her wink at Gloria and again he marvelled at how different people were to what you expected them to be when their real natures were allowed to be seen.

'We'll still wait until after the funeral, okay. I appreciate what you are thinking but I still want my family around me for the next little while. Okay?' Gloria pleaded.

'That's fine honey, but if you both change your minds, just let me know.'

12

It was Monday and the work week was about to start. John walked into the kitchen feeling very nervous. His mother and Liz were already there and so, surprisingly, was his grandmother, all dressed and looking like she was going somewhere important. 'Good morning. I'll just have coffee, please mum. I don't think I could eat anything. I've called a board meeting for nine and I'm not sure what the outcome of it is going to mean for me, or Dad for that matter.' At which point his father walked into the kitchen.

John turned to him and said, 'I'd like you to come to the office with me this morning Dad, please. I've called a board meeting at nine. I want to find out what the board wants, and I want you to hear everything that is said. After that we will make an appointment with the funeral directors. Mum, I'll let you know what time it is once I've rung them, and we will meet you there.'

'Actually, do you mind if I come as well. I know enough about the business to know that when Harry died, I get to have a say in his place, and this morning I feel like having a say.' Mavis said, her tone indicating that she wasn't interested in hearing no for an answer. Ben and John both looked at Mavis in surprise. *Who is this woman, I've never met her before?* Ben thought.

'Okay...' they both replied in unison.

Talk about things being said in stereo, John thought looking at his grandmother in surprise. All these years, and he had no idea that his grandmother had an interest in the business, let alone that she could take her husband's place at the meetings. 'Mum, do you want in on this family party too? It will save you from having to drive to the funeral director's office on your own.'

'Yeah, why not? The more the merrier by the sounds of it. Give me five to go and get ready.'

'Oh, wow, wouldn't I like to be a fly on the wall of that meeting, but I have to go and do some real work. I'll see you all tonight.' Liz said as she followed her mother out.

****

John entered the board room, while his father, mother and grandmother waited in his office, or what had been Ben's office on Friday. As he walked to the head of the table, which was at the opposite end of the room, he looked around and noted with satisfaction that Trudy, who was standing just inside the door, had seen to it that there were two extra chairs at the table.

Nine faces looked at him, belligerently, so John took the upper hand.

'Gentlemen, before we start this meeting, I want to bring in some people who have a very important stake in what will happen here today. As you have all been told, Harry died of a stroke in the early hours of Saturday morning. I have been informed, and I have no reason to doubt the information, that his place should now be filled by his wife. As my father was voted out without his knowledge, it is important to me that he too is present. As an extra witness, my mother, Harry's daughter, has also decided that she would like to be part of this meeting. Are there any objections?'

No one moved, they continued to watch him carefully.

'Alright then, Trudy, would you be kind enough to show our guests in, please.'

Trudy left the room. Two minutes passed and still no one moved or said anything, finally, Trudy returned followed by the rest of the family. They each sat down. Mavis sat in the place that Harry had occupied for years. How did she know that was his chair? *Obviously, there is some history here that I have no idea about,* thought John. As prearranged, Ben walked up and took the chair beside John and Gloria sat in the spare chair that was next to her mother. When they were comfortable, John spoke again.

76

'Well, the first order of business is to discuss the circumstances under which I was voted in as Chairman on Friday. I have to say that I wasn't surprised, but that I am not happy about the way it was carried out. I always understood that my father would at least be present when the vote was taken and that there would be a good reason why a vote of no confidence would be tabled.'

Mavis raised her hand. 'Permission to speak, Chairman'. John nodded.

'Gentlemen, I was David's secretary before I married Harry, and let me tell you, I am under no illusions about Harry and his business dealings, the man could be ruthless, particularly if you crossed him. He was very good at jumping to the wrong conclusions and I believe that the reason he wanted Ben removed was a result of him doing exactly that. What he presented to you as his reason, most likely had nothing remotely to do with the truth. I doubt he presented you with his fanciful notion that Ben was an adulterer, because you all know that it wouldn't have a legal leg to stand on. Now that he is gone, I'm sure that the family are not in the least bit interested in knowing what it was he presented to you, however, he is no longer in a position to bully any of you anymore. I'm going to suggest that Trudy and Gloria organise tea and biscuits to be bought in and you all take the time to rethink your decision.' John nodded, and Gloria and Trudy silently left the room as his grandmother continued. 'After that, if it is acceptable to the chair, I suggest the board takes another vote about who should be chairman of this business. When I have discussions with my solicitor, after the funeral, I'll be looking into the process that took place to replace David all those years ago, and if I find, and I suspect that I will, that there was an illegal removal back then, I will be back and have that motion rescinded as well. Am I understood? Gentleman, you are warned. This company was started by David and was built based on honesty, hard work, and good service. These qualities haven't been evident for some time and while I wasn't in a position to do anything about it until now, I will endeavour to see that this business lifts its game from now on. It has been a poor reflection on our family for many years and I want it fixed.'

John looked at Mavis stunned and noticed that the rest of the people in the room appeared to be in a state of shock. This lady was a force to be reckoned with. As Trudy and Gloria entered the room with a trolley loaded with tea, coffee, mugs, and biscuits, one man raised his hand.

'Yes, Barry, do you have a question?' John said.

'I'm just wondering why this woman is making such a fuss about how the business is performing. Anyone would think she had a personal stake in it.'

'That is exactly right, Barry. I do have a personal stake in this business. David gifted me a substantial amount of stock as a wedding gift when I married Harry. It was his way of saying thanks for all the work I did to help set up the business in the first place. Just because no-one was told, doesn't make it less true. Now, let's have that break while you all consider what should be done.' Mavis was the first to stand and take a mug of tea from Trudy.

During the break, Mavis, John, Ben, and Gloria left the room to allow the board members to talk freely. After about fifteen minutes they all returned to the board room and John moved that the motion to remove Ben be rescinded, the vote was unanimous. Ben took the chair and moved that John be given the position of Vice-Chairman; the vote was passed unopposed.

'Gentlemen, I thank you for your attendance today. We have a lot of work ahead of us, but right now, my family have a funeral to organise, and I think you would appreciate that we will need some time to work through the emotional and legal issues in front of us. I've asked Jack Buchannan to be acting manager while I am away on compassionate leave. Any questions?' Every man around the table shook their head silently. 'Alright then, I declare the meeting closed and I will bid you good-day.' Ben stood up and the family followed him out.

'Well, that went better than I expected.' John said as they reached the carpark. Gloria looked at her mother, and with a smile said. 'Who are you? What did you do with my mother? That was very impressive Mum. I never knew you had it in you.'

'Oh, I knew David before I met your father. If he hadn't already been married to Elizabeth, I would have happily set my sights on him back then. However, he was, and I could see from the first day Harry came into the business that he could be trouble for David.'

'So, why on earth did you marry him?' Gloria asked, puzzled.

'I actually saw it as a way to keep an eye on what was happening, which I did, but Harry never knew, he didn't have a clue. He probably would have divorced me if he had. For all his business nous he was clueless about people.

****

'So how did the board meeting go? Liz asked as they sat down that night at dinner.

'Your grandmother was very impressive.' Gloria said. 'Very impressive indeed. I didn't know who that woman in the board room was.'

'Why, what happened?'

'Oh, she told them that she knew that Harry had bullied them into doing what they had done and that now he couldn't do that anymore, they should rethink the vote and that she is going to investigate the removal of my dad.' Ben added.

'Dad was put back in as Chairman and I was voted Vice.' John said.

'Way to go, brother'

'Hey, I had nothing to do with it, Grandma did all the talking, trust me. We even discovered that she would have married David if he had been available.'

'Hey, what?'

'David wasn't available, so I married the next best option, Harry. But don't get me wrong people, even though it looked like a business arrangement, we fitted together well. He was besotted with me, and I knew it and I worked out very early in the piece how to get him to do what I knew was the right thing and that way I was able to protect the business a little bit from the sidelines.'

'What do you mean?'

'Well, I worked out that if I told him something was a good idea, he would decide that it wasn't worth doing, but if I said something was a bad idea then that would be the thing he'd fight tooth and nail for. That's how John ended up with Jack as his mentor. I appeared so outraged that Jack was even a possibility that Harry decided that he was the only person for the job. I knew that Jack was the right person, and I was determined to make sure that he got the task. There was only one time that this strategy didn't work and that was when he decided to remove David from the board. It didn't matter how many times I said it was a good idea he was determined to put Ben at the helm. I think he thought you were putty in his hands.'

'I was,' Ben said sadly.

I remember the day you were born, Ben. Your father came back to work just after lunch. He had a grin from ear to ear and every time I walked past his office door, he was either spinning around in his chair or staring out the window in a world of his own. I was so envious of your mother and you. I really was.'

'Does dad know any of this?'

'Ben, are you crazy, of course not and don't you dare breathe a word of it to him either, or I'll have you removed again from your office.' Mavis said, but Ben could see that she was smiling.

'But how did you manage to keep tabs on the business, you never went into the office?'

'Oh, that was easy. When Harry was stressed and that was a lot of the time, he would talk in his sleep. I often had whole business conversations with him during the night and he wouldn't remember a thing in the morning. I also read everything that he bought home after he went to sleep, which was mostly confidential stuff that he didn't want anyone else to get their hands on. I learnt an awful lot by just keeping my mouth shut and my eyes and ears open.'

'Well, Mavis, I believe you have been an angel hiding in plain sight and I thank you.'

'I realise now, that dad treated you badly in public. You might as well have been invisible.' Gloria said.

'Well, being invisible worked for me, it meant that I could hear and see things without people being aware that I knew what they were talking about. God helped me a lot over the years. Don't get me wrong, I had some bad times when I would cry to God and ask him "how long?" This isn't over yet. There are still a lot of bridges that have to be rebuilt carefully.'

'I just wished I had treated Mum and Dad better.'

'Well, that was hard for you to do while Harry was pulling the strings as hard as he was at the time, telling him that it was a good idea to turf them out of the house worked there too, at least until your mum died. I told him that it would let people know just how nasty he could be, there was something in his past that made it very important that people thought highly of him, even when he was behaving like a bully. I know, it didn't make sense to me either, but it usually worked. He'd already had your father's stuff removed before I knew anything had been done. So, I wasn't always as clever as I would like to believe.'

'I wondered why he was suddenly on board with them staying there. Here I was thinking that he had actually conceded to my wishes. I'm shattered,' he laughed. 'Patrick believes that he made his peace with God before he died so we will most likely see him again in Heaven.'

'You can't help your mum anymore, God is doing that, but you can help your dad. I want to help you go through the records and work out how much the business owes your dad and work out how to give it back to him. It won't make up for everything that he lost and all the years of pain but it's the least the company can do.

'I wonder what it was that made him so mean though', Liz muttered.

'Most likely his father was a bully as well, I never met the man, but there is a saying, like father, like son. The Bible also says something about the sins of the father being passed down through the generations, but we can make a choice to break the circle.'

'But didn't you perpetuate his bad behaviour by telling him that he would be a force not to be trifled with? Wouldn't it have been better to try and change him into a better person?'

'Ben, I know it seems like that, but I worked with what I had. You can't change a person; it has to be their choice. I always hoped that he would see that things didn't have to be done the way he did them. I encouraged better people to be around us, but in the end, that didn't work either. However, I really was praying very hard that this take-over thing wouldn't happen. It appears that those prayers have been answered.'

'Mum, what? Are you saying that you were praying for dad to die?' Gloria sounded horrified and tears start to run down her face.

'Oh, goodness me, Gloria. Absolutely not. I try not to tell God how to do His job. I'll admit that I sometimes try out different scenarios, but I couldn't even imagine how God was going to fix this one. I know that His imagination is so much greater than mine and that He had an answer. I just prayed and trusted that He would do something amazing.'

'It's early days yet, but I'm hopeful, that through this, God will heal our family. Sorry Gloria, I know that it's hard to have to lose your father for that to happen, but if Patrick is right, you will see him again in Heaven.' Ben said as he wrapped his arms around his wife and let her cry.

13

The funeral was on Friday afternoon; the business closed for the afternoon so those who wanted to attend could and those who wanted to have some time for themselves were able to. The family were under no illusions as to the level of affection the staff had for Harry. In the office he was a bully, and many people could never understand how Mavis lived with him. Surprisingly, most staff members attended, which Mavis said proved that they respected both Ben and John a lot. The only other people outside of the business to attend the funeral were Patrick, Jo, and David. Ben watched his father smile when he briefly greeted Mavis. *They look good together*, he thought.

****

Nobody managed to get to the kitchen until ten O'clock the next morning. Once they had arrived home, they had sat down and talked long into the night. It was decided that Mavis, John, and Liz would move back to the big house the next day. Not that there was much to do, the kids only had to pack some clothes and a few of their personal things that they wanted to take with them.

David, Patrick, and Jo were coming for Sunday lunch so they would be back for that. Mavis had warned the family that they were not to let on that she had liked David all those years ago and they had agreed, besides it was too soon after Harry's death for her to think about anyone else being in her life. He might have been a bully to others, but she had loved him in her own way, and she needed time to work through the mess he had left behind.

The family left around midday just as the rain started to fall in buckets. Ben looked at Gloria. 'Well, that puts an end to us having our special date of fish and chips beside the river.'

'How about we get fish and chips, light the fire, and have it in our living room.'

'You'd be happy with that?'

'Yes, really. Fancy things were important to Dad, and I wanted to please him by getting those things for myself. Weird I know, and it's no excuse but that's the way it was. For the first time in my life, I can relax and not keep worrying about what he is going to say.'

'Okay, then. I'll light the fire; the house could use warming up now that it's raining.'

Ben noticed Gloria smile and wondered about this woman that he had been married to for so long and was suddenly finding out so many new things about.

Early in the evening, Ben returned home from collecting the fish and chips to find Gloria sitting on the floor in front of the fire. The coffee pot and mugs were sitting on a tray on the tiles in front of it, but he couldn't take his eyes off her. She was dressed in red, however, that negligee was sending him a very clear message. He put the package down on the floor and bent down and kissed her. She wrapped her arms around his neck.

'What about the fish and chips?'

'They can wait, we can always heat them up in the microwave later.'

'So, do I make love to you here, in front of the fire, or would you prefer the bedroom?'

'The bedroom please, this floor feels much harder than it used to,' she smiled.

'Okay, then.' He bent down, lifted her up, thankful that she had taken care of herself since having had the twins and weighed no more than she had on their wedding night. and carried her upstairs to their bedroom.

'I hope you weren't going to wear that on our date to the riverbank, he whispered in her ear.

'No, but I didn't see the point in wearing the one I had purchased for that when there was no way we were going down there in the rain.'

It was obvious that Gloria had planned things very well because the bedcovers had been pulled back. He gently placed her on the bed and joined her. Afterwards, Ben lay there with Gloria cradled against his shoulder. Loving her had never been this good before. There were miracles happening all round him and he was having trouble getting his head around it all. He wondered how long these good times would last. There was still a long way to go before everything was back on the right track. While his previous journey was like being on an express way with very few exits, this road had lots of bends and turns and many more points where it would be easy to get off and reconnect with that old way. *God help us all stay on this narrow road and keep us safe as we travel along it.*

"Ask, and it will be given you. Seek, and you will find. Knock, and it will be opened for you." *There was that voice again. Thank you, Lord.* Gloria stirred, 'Are you ready for those fish and chips yet?' He asked with a smile.

'Yes, I'll probably have to make a new pot of coffee as well.'

'Okay, I'll fix the fire while you fix the coffee.' Ben dressed and moved downstairs. Gloria emerged not long after, wearing a red dressing gown. *Man, I like that colour on her. At least we don't have to get up early in the morning.* He thought.

****

John drove the three of them back to his parents' place around ten on Sunday morning.

'I wonder how mum and dad got on being in the house all by themselves last night. It would have been the first time they have ever been alone since we were born. I'm surprised they are still married; most couples would have divorced by now.'

'Neither of them would have been game for fear of what Harry would do, I guess, but don't you worry about your parents. I have a good feeling about them?' Mavis contended.

Once they reached the front door, John was surprised at the amount of noise Mavis made, however, they found their parents sitting at the kitchen table, his mother sitting on his father's lap, drinking coffee. His mother made a move that looked as if she was going to get up, but he saw his father's arm holding her back indicating to her to stay put.

'You guys just got up? John asked surprised.

'No, we have been up for a while, but the house was so quiet without you lot that we slept in and decided to just take our time having breakfast.'

'You had a good night then?' Mavis asked.

'The best.' They both replied together, Liz dug him in the ribs, John looked at his grandmother and parents and then the penny dropped.

'Oh, okay. Glad to see you guys didn't kill each other then.'

'Can you all help us get lunch ready now, please. I've planned roast lamb and vegetables, the meat is on, the vegs just need to be prepared and put on soon. Gloria's voice was very sharp and there was a pause, 'Sorry, that came out wrong. I told Patrick about twelve-thirty for lunch.'

'It's okay, Mum, just get back up and we will move forward.' John said.

There was a hive of activity as they worked, even if the conversation was a little bit clumsy, this was new territory for all of them and they were all trying to feel their way carefully.

The front doorbell rang at twenty past twelve. The whole family moved into the foyer as Ben opened the door and shook his father's hand, Liz moved forward kissed his cheek, leaving Mavis, Gloria, and John standing awkwardly behind them. Patrick was next and Ben shook his hand and Liz gave Jo a hug. Ben stepped back and turned to the rest of the family.

'Dad, you remember Gloria,'

'Hi dad,' she replied shyly. David stepped forward, took her by the shoulders and looked her up and down. 'You are as beautiful as ever, and you look well.'

'Thank you.'

'Mavis,' David moved to her mother. 'I didn't get a chance to say so the other day but I'm sorry about the death of Harry. I know you loved him, and I guess there's a big hole in your life right now. It will get easier with time.'

'Thank you, David. I appreciate you saying that.'

David then turned his attention to his grandson. 'John, my boy, oh how you have grown. I watched you at the funeral and I have to say that the man I saw there looked pretty impressive. You seemed to have matured into a fine young man.'

'Oh, Pops. I'm sorry. It was a really stupid and mean thing to do that day.'

'What day?' His grandfather smiled. 'I know, I'm sorry, I shouldn't tease. You were a kid, trying to impress your father and that often causes us to do silly things when we have misguided opinions about what might impress someone we love. I'm glad that you have seen the error of your ways and that you have had the courage to say you are sorry. That is also a sign of maturity. Can I add though, just like Joseph, what you meant for evil, God allowed for good. If I hadn't been arrested that day, I would most likely still be living on the street and I would never have met my cousin. That night in the cell was the first time I'd felt really safe in two years.'

'I never knew you had a cousin, Dad.' Ben stated.

'I met him once when I was ten years old. He was a baby in a basinet. He latched onto my finger and made baby noises at me. That was the moment I knew that one day I wanted to be a father. A good father, but I failed there, I guess.'

'Some sons are just bad sons; I was one of them.'

'Come on people, let's head into the dining room before the food gets ruined.' Gloria exclaimed.

'Good idea,' Ben said as he moved around the group and showed them into a prettily decorated dining room.

'You have a beautiful house,' Jo said to Gloria.

'It was mostly my father's vision; a beautiful house doesn't always make for a loving home though, however, from now on I plan to make some happy memories here, starting with a good meal with all the family. Take a seat wherever you feel comfortable. Liz, you want to give me a hand please?'

They returned shortly with trays of food, Ben had been busy filling glasses with soft drinks and Gloria smiled. *I like this Ben.*

Over the meal, Mavis and David reminisced about the early days when they were setting up the business. Mavis mentioned the day Ben was born. David remembered that one day, Cassidy, who had taken Mavis' place after she had married Harry, had come into his office almost laughing. David had asked her what was so funny, and she had told him that Ben, who was toddling around the office, had scribbled stuff on some spare paper and asked her to check if his sums were right. "They weren't even numbers, but I pretended that he had made lots of money. It was so cute." You could scarcely hold a pencil.' David grinned at his son.

It was a relaxed meal, and the conversation was kept light. It seemed an unspoken decision that this was not a time to get into the heavy things of the relationships.

14

'Ben, can I ask you something?' It had been several months now since Harry's death. David was helping Ben cook meat on the BBQ on their back pouch. The rest of the family were inside getting the rest of the meal ready.

'Yeah, sure Dad.'

'Where did I go wrong?'

'Huh?'

'What was it that I did that made you decide to take the road that you did?'

'Dad, it wasn't you, well, not really. I was an impatient naïve teenager, you wanted me to learn more slowly than I wanted, and I came across Harry, who saw that and milked it for all it was worth. Mavis says that Harry was clueless about people, but I sometimes wonder. He could spot a weakness in a person a mile off. It was a case of the wrong thing looking more attractive than the right thing. The problem was that once I had chosen that road, there was no way for me to get off it. It was a bit like an express way, the exits are few and far between and every time there looked to be one, Harry made sure that I wouldn't take it. I wanted to attend Mum's funeral, I was planning on staying out of sight, however, Harry set up a meeting for me at exactly the same time. I knew that it was deliberate to prevent me from going.'

'The business seems to be in good shape financially, so he must have taught you something.' David said as Patrick joined them.

'It's looks better than it is, really. The loss of customers because of Harry's dealings and the lack of good customer service are really starting to hurt our bottom line. Dad, would you consider coming back and doing an assessment of what we need to do to fix this?'

'How long do you think it would take?'

'With your skills and the foundation knowledge of the business, John thinks you could do it in two weeks.'

'Well, I've got a couple of weeks leave due. I'll run it past my boss and see if I can use that time to have a look.'

'Dad, I know you like being honest and upfront, but I'd like you to have a look around without any of the employees being aware of what you are doing. How do you feel about going undercover?'

'So, how do you think you can make that work?'

'Paul, the cleaner, is the only person who gets to work anywhere in the building without being seen. I could give him a couple of weeks off and bring you in to take his place.'

'And if anyone asks what I'm doing there?'

'Just say that Paul had to take leave and you're filling in for him. That will be the truth. I won't be giving him a choice; besides I don't think he will turn down the bonus that allows him to take his family on holidays for two weeks, do you? Please Dad, I want this fixed before it gets desperate. Harry's treatment of people got worse as he got older, and the rest of the staff lack motivation to fix things. I thought they might find a new energy without Harry around, but it just hasn't happened. I get the feeling that they don't know where to start and neither do we. This was John's suggestion and I think it's a good one. You will be getting paid the same as Paul, his bonus is coming out of my pocket for the moment. I just don't want anyone to get wind of what we are doing. When you've worked out what we need to do, then I'd like you to help us formulate a plan but that can be done on the weekends.'

'Alright. Alright. I'll talk to my boss on Monday and let you know. I guess you'd need a couple of weeks to set this up right?'

'Yeah, that would be handy.'

'Okay, I'll talk to you on Monday night then.'

****

A month later, David, Ben, and John were sitting around Ben's dining table. It was a Sunday night and the family had gathered for what was now a regular meal together. Tonight, had been warm enough to have a BBQ again, but the men had left the women outside while they discussed the results of David's undercover work. 'Gentlemen, you have a number of problems but there is one that is I see as being at the top of the list.'

'Dad, we know that but what are they?'

'It's simple, your staff don't trust each other, they have no idea how to talk nicely, or how to work together. They have been listening to Harry for so long that they all sound and behave like him. I suggest that Mavis be employed to try and retrain the secretarial staff; Jack is probably the best person to try and mentor the executives. I almost want to suggest that you start a choir, make everyone sing, just to get some variation in their voices and help them to learn to work as a team not as competitors.'

'And the others?'

'There's some sexual harassment going on, particularly in Barry Stones' department and just not the staff, customers are being treated badly as well; the other one is customer service but a lot of that will be fixed when you fix the first two.'

'Are you sure you don't want to come back to the office full-time?'

'I've enjoyed being around the place for the last couple of weeks, but I like working with the men and it does help keep me fit. I'll think about it though. Would you be happy if I only came into the office for a couple of days a week?'

'Yes Dad, anything will help at this point.'

'I'll have to talk to Terry, my boss, and see what we can work out then.'

****

'David, can I see you in my office before you start, please?' Terry said as he was signing in. It was Monday morning and the conversation with Ben and John the night before was still very much in his thoughts.

'Sure, what's up?'

'David, you are a very valuable worker and I count it a privilege to have been able to assist you to get back on your feet. However, I have been approached by a mate to try and do the same thing I have done for you for a friend of theirs. I was wondering if you would be willing to give up a couple of days a week for about three months so I can give this guy a go. The problem is that is if he proves himself, I'll kinda need to put him on full-time after the three months. He's a much younger man and has a family to raise. Do you see my dilemma?'

'Oh, boy.' David said quietly.

'David, I'm sorry.'

'No, it's fine. Ben and John have been pushing me to go back to the office and I'd be happy to give up the couple of days to start with as I also want to ease my way back into the office and work out how to maintain my fitness levels. That's been the best thing about working here really, apart from the fellowship with the men. I think you call this a case of before you ask, God has an answer.'

'Well, thank you, as I said, and I really mean it, it's been a privilege to work with you and see you back on your feet. It's also good to know that things are working out with your family, you deserve a break after all you have been through.'

'I am really grateful to you and if you can give the next guy a leg-up then I'm happy to step aside and help that happen.'

'Great, he will be starting next week, so how about you take Tuesdays and Thursdays off.'

'Sounds good to me. I'd better get out there and do something now though or the boys will think I'm shirking, and we can't have that!'

'True, thanks again and I'll talk to you again when I know more about how this guy is shaping up. See you later.'

15

Two weeks later Ben, David and John were in the office talking about how best to fix a string of the smaller business problems when Trudy knocked on the door and entered without waiting for them to answer her.

'Ben, your wife is on the phone.'

'Can't it wait, we are in the middle of an important meeting.'

'You need to take this call and I think you should put it on speaker.'

Ben looked at the other two men, fear rising in him and said 'Okay, put it through'. Two seconds later Ben heard Gloria's panicked voice. Once he would have started to groan on the inside, wondering what new drama she was cooking up this time, but something in Trudy's voice and the knowledge that Gloria was making a real effort to be a better wife, made him resolve to listen.

'Ben, Liz didn't arrive at work. Mavis is here, they rang her this morning to find out if she was sick. Mavis said that she left for work at her usual time, just after John. She didn't say anything about doing anything different this morning.'

Trudy entered the office again, indicated that David come to her at the doorway.

'There's another call on line two The caller says that he is calling about the kidnapping of Liz.'

David quickly returned to the desk. 'Gloria, Mavis, there's a call on line two that we need to take, we will ring you straight back, in the meantime, I suggest you make yourselves a cuppa and pray for Liz's safety. John will be there as soon as we know what the other caller wants.' David interrupted as he cut the call and put the new call on speaker. *Old habits die hard,* he thought, as he realised that he was taking over without Ben or John's permission, but they were both looking pretty stressed. Having not had a very long relationship with his granddaughter seemed to help him stay a little more objective.

'Gentlemen, I have Liz here with me. I have been instructed to ask for one hundred thousand dollars or', the men exchanged startled looks,.... 'I'll let your imagination work out what happens to her.'

'I want to speak to my granddaughter'. David's voice seemed calm and professional.

'Pop. I love you,' they heard the stress in her voice.

'Have they hurt you?'

'No, not yet, but Pop I just want to say that I'm sorry for stabbing you all those years ago.'

'That's enough of the family chit chat. You have one hour to convince the bank to give you the money. I'll ring you with instructions then.' The line went dead.

'Okay, that's odd, she didn't stab me. The only time that I came close to being stabbed was when you, John, pretended to do it the day I ended up in the Police cells, why would she say she did it? She had disappeared before the Police arrived.'

'Oh, I think she's trying to say that she thinks she's in Lillydale. That's where we were that day.'

'John, I think you need to get home and look after your mother and grandmother. Tell them what has happened. We are about to ring Patrick to see what he can do'. Ben looked at his son. 'I know it will be hard for you to go home and not to be here helping us, but we will ring you as soon as we know something, please try and keep the women as calm as you can'.

'Sure, Dad. I'll do my best.'

Ben started to ring Patrick's home number. He looked at David, 'let's hope he isn't on duty'. Jo answered after what seemed to be an age.

'Jo, is Patrick home.'

'Yeah, I'll get him for you.' Ben couldn't help but tap his foot while he waited for Patrick to come onto the line.

'Patrick, would you mind coming to the office, but we need you to come here in plain clothes, it appears that Liz has been kidnapped.'

'I'm on my way,' and the line went dead.

Within ten minutes, Patrick turned up looking dirty and scruffy, he had clearly been gardening when Jo had called him to the phone.

'Okay, guys what do we know?' Ben and David retold the story of the phone call, Liz's strange words, and John's conclusion that she was trying to give them some idea of where to start looking for her. They also mentioned that the crook had told them they had one hour to convince the bank to give them the amount of one hundred thousand dollars.

'Well, we aren't dealing with some very bright characters then. Who have you had problems with here in the last little while?'

'I've had to speak to Barry Stone a couple of times. There have been a number of complaints about the way he is treating his staff, particularly his female members. I told him last week that if he didn't start to make some changes, I'd have to reconsider his position in the business, but why are you so sure it's an inside job.'

'Simple, if it was someone not related to the business, they would assume that you had that sort of money available without having to convince the bank to give it to you. I remember you saying at our BBQ a couple of months back that things look better than they are in reality. This has to be organised by someone who knows what the real state of affairs is.'

'Okay, but that still doesn't help us actually find her. It's not like we can accuse Barry of doing something without finding her first otherwise things might get nasty.'

'Yeah, I know, try to stay calm. I understand that you have fears for Liz, but...'

'You don't have kids; how can you know!'

'Ben, come on son, stay with us here. Patrick is trying to help. Getting upset will not help Liz or us in finding her.' David reached out and place his hand on Ben's shoulder.

'I'm sorry. I just don't know what I'd do if this guy hurts her. What if he raped her?'

'Ben, trust God to look after her. There's no need to borrow trouble from tomorrow. We will deal with it if and when it happens. Pray that He will protect her. He protected David for the two years he was living on the streets, so protecting her isn't going to be beyond His means. If something goes wrong than we will have to rely on the strength He gives to get her through the recovery. I'm going to ring a buddy of mine. I remember him saying something about an empty warehouse showing signs of being disturbed the other day.'

He picked up the phone. 'Thomas, can you tell me where that warehouse was that you thought might have had some activity around it the other day.'

The conversation carried on for a few minutes in which Patrick told Thomas about what they had suspected might have happened. Finally, Patrick said, 'I'll see you there.' And he hung up.

'Is Barry at work today?'

'I'll ask Trudy', Ben left the room returning shortly afterwards nodding.

'Okay, can you guys come up with something that you can have a meeting with him over. Nothing to do with his behaviour. I want you to keep him occupied for about an hour. So, if you have some new plans that you can convince him that you need his input on, it would be helpful. That way this guy can be dealt with, without him getting any idea of what is going down.' Ben and David looked at each other.

'There were those extension plans that we are going to put on hold for a while, what if we tell him that we need his input on them before we consider going ahead with them.'

'Sounds plausible, I just need him busy for the next hour at least. You only have a half hour left before they ring back with your instructions, I'm hoping that we can get to them before that time is up. The extra time will give us time to get them to the station. I'll ring Trudy as soon as Liz is safe. Get her to deliver the message to you on paper. You can then deal with Barry as you see fit. We should be able to find out from his henchman if he is the orchestrator of this little rumble. If not then we'll have to do some more work.'

David and Ben walked into Barry's office. Ben placed the plans on Barry's desk and the look on Barry's face, left them in no doubt that he was in fact up to no good.

'Barry, we need you to have a look at these plans and let us know what you think about them and suggest any changes you think might make them better.'

'Are you sure this is necessary to do right now? Haven't you got something else more important to do?'

'Like what?' They both said together, looking at each other as if they were completely mystified.

'Um, nothing. Let's have a look at those plans.'

Fifteen minutes later, there was a knock at Barry's office door. 'Come in' he said, this time it was his turn to look mystified.

'Good afternoon, Mr Stone, how are you today.' However, it wasn't Trudy who had entered the room, but Liz herself. It took everything Ben had, not to race to her and hug her. Patrick was standing right behind her, and he sent them a warning sign to stay calm. 'Are you surprised to see me? Your henchman was silly enough to talk to me the whole time he held me. Man, can he talk. These officers are here to arrest you for my kidnapping.'

Patrick was still dressed in his gardening clothes, but another officer in uniform stepped forward and put handcuffs on him.

'How can you do this to me, you're my son?' Barry pleaded with the officer.

'You broke the law, my job comes first, you taught me that in good measure.'

'Why?' Ben directed the question to Barry.

He shrugged his shoulders, 'I love my job and you were going to take it away from me, so I took something you love. After all she is only a girl of no consequence, something to play with.'

'WHY YOU....' Ben moved towards Barry ready to punch him. David and Patrick, both restrained him, as Thomas also put his hand up, his palm against Ben's chest. 'He's not worth it', they all said together.

'Consider yourself sacked.' Ben yelled at him as he turned and hugged Liz, 'Did he touch you?'

'No, he was too silly for that. He made threats but really, he was more scared of you than him.' She nodded in Barry's direction. 'I told him Barry wouldn't pay him, even if he managed to get hold of the money. Besides it turned out I was fitter than him anyway. He is sporting some pretty good bruises. All those fights that John and I had as kids made me very capable of defending myself.'

'That's why we were so fast getting back. She had managed to tie him up, bundled him into her boot and was bringing him back here when we came across them. She was driving like a bat out of hell, with hazard lights going, which meant that any police car was going to pick her up for speeding. We had informed all the cars around that we were looking for her car as well.' This young officer was the first man on the scene and was able to apprehend the guy properly.'

'You have an amazing daughter there Mr Banister.' Thomas said. 'Come on you. You have an appointment with a judge, along with your mate, after a night in the cells.'

'Patrick, would you please bring that officer to our place for lunch as soon as you both have a Sunday off. I want to thank him properly for helping my daughter.'

'Thank you, sir I would like that', the officer said looking back at Liz, as he continued through the door.

'Alright, we need to get you home and let the rest of the family know that you are safe. I think we can take the rest of the day off. I'll tell Trudy we are going home.'

There were hugs and smiles as soon as the family arrived home. They found that Jo had arrived and had prepared lunch.

'What I don't understand is how this guy was able to grab you in the first place.' John looked at his sister.

'He had the element of surprise. When I drove out after you this morning his car was parked across the road. I had to stop because there was no way around it. He told me he had a flat tyre and could he borrow my jack. I opened the boot and he pushed me in and closed the lid.'

'Come to think of it, there has been several mornings when I've noticed a car on that road. It seemed strange but it was always a different car parked in a different place.' John reflected.

'There has been a spat of what we thought were joy riders, taking cars and leaving them a few houses away. One fellow ran into the station to tell us that he had left the keys in his car overnight and when he came out in the morning, he'd put his hand on the bonnet and noticed that it was warm. If it was this guy using these cars to case your routine then he really had a cheek, taking the guy's car and putting it back in his driveway.'

'Yes, I noticed them as well, but didn't think any more about them either. Tuesday is the only day that you leave for work before me and so I'm guessing that he wasn't going to try on a day when you might come down the road after me before he got away. Anyway, when we got to Lillydale, I played along because I knew that he wasn't working on his own and we needed to find out who was behind it.'

'How did you figure out that's where you were?'

'Oh, easy enough, I know how long it takes to get there and the other towns around are either closer or further out. I've driven over there enough to know what the road is like; the rattly bridge was also a pretty big give away.'

'You sounded so stressed' Ben said.

'Oh, so I was convincing then?'

'Very.'

'I knew it was going to be hard on you guys but if I carried on as if I wasn't scared then I may not have been able to convince him that I wouldn't fight back. I needed him to think I was weak in order to get him to untie my ropes. It also gave me time to scan the place and see what my options were. Sorry, I didn't want to worry you, but I knew that you would work out where I was when I talked about stabbing you, Pop.'

'John worked that out.'

'Well so he should have, after all he was there and it was his stunt, not mine.' This made everyone giggle. 'So, once he undid the ropes, I managed to land some good punches in some strategic places we were taught about in self-defence classes at school. While he was down, I tied him up and returned the favour of putting him in my boot. Job done! I knew that if I drove fast with the hazards going someone would pick up the message that I needed help, and they did.'

'I'm just glad you weren't hurt,' her father said with feeling.

'I'm glad we were able to work out that Barry was behind it and good riddance to bad rubbish if you ask me. I'm glad you sacked him Dad.'

Patrick had been listening and watching this amazing young woman, 'Have you ever thought of joining the Police force, Liz?' Patrick finally said as there was a lull in the conversation.

'Please don't!' Ben and Gloria said together.

'I know you are a very capable girl, but I don't want to deal with that sort of stress ever again and it would be a daily thing if you worked in law enforcement. Sorry Patrick, find a new recruit somewhere else, please,' Ben smiled to take the edge off his words.

'Point taken, but Liz, seriously, if you change your mind, you have the sort of skills that we need,' Patrick said.

'Thanks Patrick but I am very happy doing what I am at the moment at least.'

'Alright, fair enough. I think it's time that we returned home and left you all to have some down time and recuperate. We'll see you all again on Sunday if not before. If there is anything else that you need, you know where to find us.'

'Okay guys, I'll see you both in the office tomorrow,' David said as he moved towards the front door, following Patrick and Jo. Suddenly David stopped and turned around to Ben and John. 'Oh, by the way, I'm sorry about taking over back there. It's your business still and I shouldn't have done that.'

'Dad, its fine, I didn't even realise you'd done that. I guess I was panicking too much to notice.'

'Thanks son, I'll try to be more careful in the future. Bye.' and the door closed behind him.

'Gran, can we go home as well, I need a shower. I might have cleaned out my boot recently, but I still feel grubby. I'd better ring work and let them know that I'm okay.'

'Already done, dear,' Mavis said, 'and they said they'll see you tomorrow.'

'Oh, thank you Gran, you're the best.' Liz enthused as she hugged her grandmother.

The house was suddenly very quiet again. 'I need another cup of coffee, and I truly don't want to feel that scared ever again.' Ben looked at Gloria's face which was still showing signs of stress, 'you either?'

'No, I certainly don't. I guess we should thank God that he was looking after her and made sure she had the skills to deal with the situation.'

'Yes, I think you are right there. Here, let's go into the lounge and drink our coffees. It's easier to relax in there.' Ben placed his arm around his wife and led her into the other room. Despite the trauma of the events that day, he again marvelled at how calm they both were. If this had happened pre-Harry's death, he knew that the blame game would have been played to the fullest extent of its possibilities and he would have been culprit number one.

Thank you, Lord, for helping us in this healing process, he prayed silently.

16

The phone shrilled indicating that Trudy wanted to speak to him. John answered. It had been a month since the day Liz had been kidnapped, and life seemed to be getting back to normal again, whatever that was. The family hadn't even managed to get together for their regular Sunday lunches as the men tried to sort out how to fix the business.

'Yes, Trudy.'

'There's a Mandy Stone here. She would like to see you and your father. I've spoken to him; he is on his way in.'

'Okay, send her in.'

John stood up just as his father entered through the other door of his office. Ben had moved into Harry's old office as it was a bigger space and had a much better view.

'I wonder what this is about', his father said quietly.

'I guess we are about to find out,' he replied as the door opened and in walked a slim, blond girl, about John's age, wearing a neat trouser suit.

Man, she is beautiful. John thought.

'How can we help you?' Ben said, bringing John back to his senses.

'I'm sorry, gentlemen, I'm Barry Stones' daughter.'

Oh, here's trouble. I should have known things that look too good to be true usually are.

'I just wanted to say on behalf of myself, my brother, and my mother that we are sorry for what my father tried to do to your family. We know that we're not responsible for his actions but just wanted you to know that if there is anything that we can do to help, to please let us know. None of us are sure what we might be able to do as you have to understand that things are difficult for us right now. I was let go from my job and my mother has filed for divorce, hence, she wasn't able to come with me.

How is your daughter Mr Banister, I hope there were no physical injuries?'

'Thank you, she does seem to be fine.'

'Oh, so you think we owe you a job because we let your father go?' John heard himself saying suspiciously.

'No, sir. That wasn't my intention at all. I know that my father has hurt you all as he has hurt us. My mother in particular wanted you to know that she wasn't party to his scheme and only heard about it after he was arrested. To say that she feels embarrassed is putting it mildly. She also asked me to come here today to find out if there is any indication that he had taken any funds unlawfully from the business because, if that is found to be the case, we will need to know how much so we can find some way to reimburse you, however, I hope you understand that it may take us awhile?'

'To be honest Miss Stone, we haven't had time yet to investigate that matter, nevertheless, if you would be kind enough to leave your contact details with my secretary, we will be in touch if we find that there is something you can do.' John wanted this conversation over with. She was beautiful to look at, but boy she was here to cause trouble, of that he was certain. Like father, like daughter.

'Good day, Miss Stone.' He watched her leave the room looking dejected. *Good riddance.*

'John, you were being a bit unfair, what got into you?' Ben looked at his son.

'Oh, come on dad, her father's a crook, she's going to be just like him. Trying to get her way into the business and starting to rip us off as soon as she can. I know the sort, her father was just like Harry, and he would have trained her in the same way Harry tried to train me.'

'My point exactly.'

'Huh?'

'Harry tried and failed. Let me remind you, your father was no angel either at much the same age you both are now. Are you sure that you are not taking it out on her because I didn't have the courage to stand up to Harry?'

'But Harry did all the dirty work, not you.'

'Oh, come on, John. You know as well as I do that I'm just as guilty because I didn't do anything to stop him and I have to tell you I felt pretty pleased with how things went for the first few years, until I realised that Harry didn't care about me, but was just pulling my strings. I'm as guilty as he was because I let him do it.'

'But you didn't know all that he was doing.'

'Doesn't matter. I hope you are not assuming that she hasn't got the decency to stand against her father just because she is female. Remember, one of the issues I had with Barry was that he had exactly the same attitude to women as you are expressing right now. John, please think about what you've said, and when you have, I think you need to contact that young lady and apologise to her. Our family knows better than many others that God is a God that gives second chances over and over again and He expects us to try and do the same.'

'What if I'm right?'

'What if you are wrong would be more to the point. I saw how you looked at her when she walked in. She is beautiful and if that goes more than skin deep, then I think you could be in danger of missing out on the best thing that might ever happen to you. I believe in love at first sight, remember, I fell in love with your mother the first time I laid eyes on her. Like father, like son, I'm guessing. Our marriage wasn't all it could have been up to now but mate, let me tell you, if you start out on the right foot you will be blessed beyond your dreams. It's not your fault that your mother and I got so much wrong, but things are so much better now that we are walking side by side not working against each other. Please don't make the same mistakes we did.'

After his father had left his office, John sat down at his desk, picked up a pen and just started doodling. If anyone had walked in and looked, they would have noticed that John was deep in thought and that the marks looked like a string of "M's".

He knew that he was being very unfair to Mandy, but the memories of that awful day had come flooding back along with the very sick feeling that he'd experienced that morning.

He hadn't told his father or grandfather, he hadn't even told Liz, but he had started to feel very ill just after he had got to work. He thought that he must have eaten something at breakfast that didn't agree with him. He was about to tell them that he was going home, he felt that bad, when Trudy had entered to tell them about the call. That sick feeling had stayed there even after he went home to be with his mother and grandmother. Then it suddenly went away. Somewhere in his brain, John knew that Liz was safe and that his churning stomach was related to her being in danger. With the return of that feeling this morning when Mandy had walked into his office, he had assumed that his body was telling him that she was trouble. Jack had always told him that trouble came dressed up to look enticing, increasing the temptation, just like the apple in the Garden of Eden, and Mandy had looked very enticing. *Oh, she is beautiful. Dad is right though, it's not her fault that her father tried to hurt Liz and she did come to try and work out how to make things right. That couldn't have been easy for her and what about her brother, he had to arrest his father for the same crime. What's the saying: you can pick your friends, but you are stuck with your family, or something like that. Jack did say once, God gives us family to teach us to get along with people we don't particularly like.*

John looked at the time, it was nearly lunchtime. He picked up his phone and pushed Trudy's extension. 'Can I have Miss Stone's number please.'

'Sure.' He wrote it down on a small blank spot on the page.

'Thanks Trudy, I'll be going out for lunch today, I hope, and I might be back later than usual. Do I have any appointments this afternoon that I've forgotten about?'

'No, there's nothing until tomorrow morning at ten.'

'Okay, good I'll see you this afternoon.'

'Or tomorrow morning?'

'Maybe, who knows.'

John dialled the number, Mandy answered.

'Mandy Stone, can I help you?'

'Mandy, it's John Bannister here.'

'Oh.'

'Hey, I'm sorry I was rude to you when you came into the office this morning. Would you please allow me to take you to lunch to say I'm sorry?'

'I'm not sure that is a good idea. After all, my father tried to destroy your family, aren't you afraid that I'm going to do the same thing.'

'Huh? I didn't say that.'

'John, I saw the look on your face, I could tell that you most likely think that I'm my father's daughter and will behave the same way he did.'

'Yikes.'

'Some people wear their heart on their sleeve, but you wear yours all over your face.'

'Then come to lunch and change my face, please?'

'Oh alright, as long as we go Dutch, where, and when?'

'John named a café around the corner from the office and said, 'I'll meet you there at 12.30?'

'Okay, I'll be there.'

John's stomach started to churn again. *Is this what happens when you fall in love? It's an awful feeling if it is.'*

Feeling restless, he left the office and walked around the park a few times before going into the café. He looked at his watch, he still had to wait another forty-five minutes before she would arrive, if she was on time, or even turned up at all. He ordered a coffee and sat stirring it so long that when he took a sip, it was cold. As he put the mug back down, the door opened, he looked up and there she was, still dressed in the suit she had worn to the office. John couldn't take his eyes off her as she walked towards him.

'Hello.'

'Oh, hi. Can I get you a coffee, mine's gone cold?'

'Sure. Why not.'

John got up and ordered the coffees at the counter and came back with menus in his hand.

'We can decide what we want to eat, while we wait for our coffees.'

The coffees arrived very quickly, the waitress removing John's cold one with a bit of a smile.

'I'm surprised there's a bottom in this cup, you stirred that coffee so long' she said. 'I hope you intend to drink this one.'

'I will.' And to prove it he lifted the mug straight to his lips.

'Mumm. That's a good coffee, thank you.' He said smiling at her, as his stomach started to settle down.

'You're welcome, enjoy. I'll be back in a little while to take your order.'

He turned back to Mandy. 'So, tell me about your family.'

'There's just mum, dad who is now in jail as you know, my brother, and me.' She went on to tell how her father had charmed his way into her mother's life and then turned out to be a bully even at home.

'Why didn't your mother leave him before this?'

'I asked that once, she said that she made her vows before God and that she had to trust God to protect her. Besides, when you start to try and get help, there really isn't the help available for women in her position. Most people didn't believe what he was really like because he was so charming when he was out and about. Maybe one day, people will believe that these things are true.'

'What about you?'

'What do you mean, What about me?'

'I don't know, you seem to have a strength about you that doesn't fit with being the child of a bully, that's all.'

'My faith in God. It's not easy let me tell you. I have to tell myself every day that God made me for a reason, and I have value to Him regardless of what my father tells me. Mum made sure that we knew that even when we were little. It was very hard for her, but she faithfully did what she felt God wanted her to do and right now he is giving her the break from dad that she really needs. This seems mean and it probably is, but I hope he doesn't come out of jail even if he finds salvation in there. Mum deserves some sort of happy ending to her earthly life.'

'Isn't Heaven supposed to be the reward for faithful service?'

'Yeah, maybe, but I would still like to see her have some good memories to take there with her. That sounds silly, I know, but that's how I feel about it.'

The waitress arrived to take their order. After she had left Mandy said.

'Now tell me about you, from what I've heard, Harry wasn't much better than my father and your father did the wrong thing as well.'

'Yes, that was one thing that my dad pointed out to me after you left the office this morning. I tried to make excuses for him, but he wouldn't let me. Our family has had a major turnaround in the last few months since

Harry died and that why I need to say I'm sorry for the way I treated you this morning.'

Their food arrived and they continued to eat, drink several mugs of coffee, and talk until the waitress came back to their table.

'Excuse me folks, but we close up at three, in ten minutes, is there anything I can get you to take with you.'

'Oh, wow, is that the time?' John looked at his watch.

'Haven't you got to get back to the office?'

'Not really, I don't have anything important on until tomorrow. How about we get a takeaway coffee and have it in the park, it's such beautiful weather at the moment.'

'Okay, two coffees to take away, I'll have them waiting for you at the counter when you pay on your way out.'

****

The following Sunday, the family again met to enjoy lunch together in the form of a BBQ. Ben had rung Patrick earlier in the week and asked that he not only invite Thomas, but Mandy and their mother as well, which Patrick had done gladly. He had spent a lot of time with the family since Barry's arrest and knew that they were keen to try and make amends, however, he also knew that the only way that they were going to realise that they were not being held responsible for Barry's actions was for them to spend time with the family in an informal setting.

They didn't use the front door on these occasions, Patrick led the visitors into the backyard via a side gate next to the garage. Ben had gone up to Thomas as soon as they arrived, shaking his hand firmly. 'I'm so pleased that you have been able to join us today. I understand that your family must be feeling apprehensive but believe me, we don't hold you responsible for Barry's behaviour.' Looking directly at Mandy and her mother. They responded with weak smiles.

'Thank you for inviting us, its very kind of you.' Thomas said, 'This is my mother Karen, and you have already met Mandy.'

Before Ben could respond, Gloria came out of the house with a tray of drinks. 'Please come and sit down and take a load off. What would you like to drink?'

John soon swooped on Mandy, making sure that she had a drink and some pre-lunch snacks and remained very attentive during the whole afternoon.

Thomas was leaning against the wall, looking quite uncomfortable, when Liz breezed in from the house. 'Sorry, I'm late. The reports due tomorrow took longer than I expected. Oh, Thomas, there you are, how are you? I'm glad you're here, it seems such an age since we met.' Thomas shifted his body off the wall and stood up straight. 'Hi, it's nice to see you again as well. Can I get you a drink?'

'Yes, please, I'll have a lemon squash thanks. My brain feels as if it's going to explode. I hate doing those reports, but they have got to be done.' Thomas moved quickly and soon returned with two drinks, one for Liz and one for himself.

'Paperwork can be a bore'

'Yes, let's go and sit down over there in the shade.' They moved to a seat and became deep in a conversation. David noticed that they looked very relaxed together as did John and Mandy. *It wouldn't surprise me if this is the beginning of something big and very long term.*

'Come on everyone, it's time to eat.' Gloria called and everyone moved to the central table and started to pile food on their plates.

'Wow, this is really nice.' Mandy said. 'I wish I could cook like this.'

'Oh, Mandy,' Liz said, 'Thomas was telling me that you were let go from your previous place because of the actions of your father'. Mandy shot her brother a stern look. 'He also tells me that you have a great deal of sales experience. How about you come into the shop tomorrow and I'll

111

have a chat to my boss. I know that she is looking to hire more staff soon.'

'But Liz, why? She's not going to want to hire me, not after what dad did.'

'Do you want a job?'

'Yes. Desperately.'

'Well, okay, come into the shop tomorrow and see what happens. After all, if I'm okay with hiring you, and I was the one wronged, then I don't think my boss is going to have a problem either. Second chances are worth grabbing with both hands, I say.'

17

David had been right. There were months of dating from that time on. David had noticed that they did a few things like that, made the same sort of choices without knowing that the other was doing the same, it was a twin thing he assumed, and he found it interesting to watch.

Once the twins had started dating, it wasn't unusual for Mandy and Thomas' mother, Karen to join them for Sunday lunch. Further investigations had revealed that there had been fraud. It had gone all the way back to when David had been removed by the board. Patrick's statement that they were dealing with someone who wasn't very bright turned out to be pretty accurate. It was discovered that false stock accounts had been set up and sales had been engineered by getting David's signature on what he thought was a purchase order. Most of the fraud had been committed by Harry but it had been done in such a way that it meant that Barry was left holding the bag, so to speak, and was still in jail and wasn't going to be out for some considerable time. It had even taken Mavis by surprise, and it had been hard work to prove that she had no knowledge of what had been going on.

***

It was a bitter cold winter's night, and the family were enjoying another great family dinner, when both couples had announced that they were engaged. Although the kids had been dating for only a few months, David wasn't surprised and was somewhat amused that he had called this one correctly, even if the family knew nothing about his suspicions.

Ben had known about Liz and Thomas of course; Thomas having done the traditional thing by asking Ben for his blessing. John had asked Mandy's mother a few weeks previously, but they had kept their engagement quiet until the lunch gathering.

These young people knew what they wanted and were going to get it with that same determined streak that came from previous generations. *Like father, like son, like son and daughter,* thought David.

With the announcement of their engagements and the wedding date set, Ben and Gloria's household seemed to go into overdrive. Gloria was in her element. She had the biggest party of her life to organise, and she relished the responsibility. Mavis was even caught up in all the excitement.

What had touched David, was that Mandy had asked Patrick to present her to her groom. As Thomas' senior officer, Patrick and Jo had spent a lot of time with the family to help them to come to terms with the fall-out during the investigation. Karen had become so distraught, crying tears of humiliation to the point she had made herself sick with guilt, and spent several weeks in hospital. 'How could I have lived with the man for so long and not had a clue?' she had cried when Patrick and Jo had visited her just after she had been admitted.

They were finishing their evening meal one night when Mandy had knocked on their door after having visited her mother in hospital. 'Patrick and Jo, can I please ask you both for a favour?'

'Sure, providing it's actually possible,' he smiled, 'you know that we are here for your family'. David had quietly collected a mug from the kitchen, filled it with tea and placed it in front of her. She smiled and took a long sip.

'Mum just isn't up to doing anything at the moment or even for the foreseeable future, and with dad still in jail, I was wondering if you guys would become my de-facto parents.'

'Sorry, what do you mean?' Patrick had asked surprised.

'What I mean is, will you stand in for Dad, Patrick? Would you please give me away? Liz has her father, but I wouldn't even want Dad to do it, even if he was out of jail. Please, will you walk me down the aisle? You have helped us so much since Liz's kidnapping. You've been the father to Thomas and me that my father should have been and wasn't.'

Patrick stood up, walked around the table, and hugged Mandy as if she was the daughter that he had never had the privilege to raise, tears making his eyes glisten.

'Oh, Mandy, it would be my privilege. You are an amazing young woman and if you were my daughter, I couldn't be prouder of how grown up you are'. David glanced at Jo and noticed the sadness in her eyes. He reached out and touched her hand. Mandy noticed the movement and released Patrick.

'Jo, I know that I have a mother, but she isn't capable of doing anything very much. The doctors have ordered complete bedrest even after she gets out of hospital. They are even concerned that she might not be well enough to attend the wedding. Would you be available to come shopping with me for my wedding dress next week? Mavis and Gloria have helped with the invitations, but they are, and rightly so, concentrating on what Liz wants. I have no one to actually help me. I know that's it's a joint wedding, but I would appreciate it if you could help me to do the things that I need to do so mum doesn't have to worry about anything other than to get better. I so badly want her to be well enough to actually be part of my special day but if she does too much in the meantime that might not be possible.'

'Oh, Mandy, it would be my pleasure but are you sure your mother won't be hurt if I do this?' David could see that sadness had turned to concern. 'I don't want to add to her feelings of guilt.'

Mandy had moved and squatted down beside Jo, holding her hands. 'Please help me, I haven't got a clue about what I need to do?'

Jo reached out and hugged her. 'Yes, I can help you. I will make sure that we take lots of photos to show your mum which I hope will make her feel she is as much a part of this as she can be.'

'Oh, thank you, you have no idea how much this means to me.'

'No, it's me who should be thanking you, with no daughter of my own I never thought it would be possible to share the joys and challenges of getting a daughter ready for her special day.'

Well now you have a de-facto daughter. Thank you, both of you. Now I'd better leave you to the rest of the evening. I have things to do to get ready for work in the morning.

John has a wonderful girl here. David thought. *She is so thoughtful and compassionate.*

18

The day was beautiful. The sun was shining and there wasn't a cloud in the sky, a bit like life at the moment, David thought, however, he knew that, like the weather, it wouldn't last. There would be challenges ahead, just as there would be rain and stormy days around the corner. There was no point worrying about tomorrow when today was perfect, and he was going to enjoy it.

Both brides were beautifully dressed in white, the gooms in white suits. Yes, the twins had opted for a joint wedding. The female attendants looked beautiful in dresses of blue. While Liz and Mandy had both picked the same colour for their bridesmaids they had opted for very different styles. There had been laughter all round when it was discovered that both brides wanted the same blue for their attendants, and yes, the men also wore matching blue suits. Now the reception was in full swing, the guests milling around and smiling as they admired the flowers, the table settings, and most of all the bridal parties. Mavis had ensured that the garden had been planted with every coloured flower that could be purchased. David and the gardeners Mavis had employed, had pruned, mowed, weeded, watered, and repaired everything to within an inch of its life to make sure that the twin's special day would go off without a hitch. And if what they were hearing from the guests was correct, they had succeeded.

David was again in a reflective mood but jerked back to the present as Mavis came up and stood silently beside him. He continued to watch the scene with pride and a grateful heart. God had answered his prayers. His family had been restored to him and today it was being extended further. Best of all, his family had found God. Tears started to run down his face. A hand holding a tissue touched his. 'God is good, and life is good again.' he said trying to explain the tears.

'I know. Our Father's love knows no bounds.'

'Young love is grand, isn't it? He said with a note of regret, swiping the tears away.

'Yes, but love at any age is grand, as long as God is part of the equation.' Mavis almost whispered back, 'young love is filled with expectations, dreams, and possibilities. I just pray that they will have the time and make the effort to see it mature into something enduring, stable, and companionable.' Mavis said with a wishful tone in her voice. They stood together quietly watching the crowd for a few more minutes.

'Mavis,' David's voice had an urgent note to it, 'we have always worked well together, especially these last few months getting the garden and house ready for the wedding. I have so loved watching you and hearing about all the times you shared with the grandkids over the years, something I missed out on. I wonder,…would you consider spending the rest of our lives together so we can share more of that love and create many more good memories particularly with some great grandkids.'

'David Bannister, are you asking me to marry you?'

'Yes, I am. It might seem sudden, and I haven't courted you in the way those young ones have, but hang it, Mavis, we aren't getting any younger and I don't want to waste any more time. Life is too short for that. You just said that love is grand at any age.'

'Oh, David, I would love to be able to do that.'

'But.' *Here goes, she really wants me to court her properly.*

'No, buts. That's a yes, you know.'

'Oh, wow. Really? I love you.' He bent down, cupped her face in his hands and kissed her. Life was indeed good.

Other Books by this Author

All these books, with the exception of Whispers from on High, are available as eBooks

Turning Water into Wine
100 Stories of God's Hand in Life

More Water into Wine
100 Stories of God's Hand in Life

Still More Water into Wine
100 Stories of God's Hand in Life

Reflections
Australian Stories from my Father's Past

365 Glasses of Wine
Short Devotionals for each day of the year

Conversations with Myself – Volume 1
100 Stories of Hope, Faith, and Determination

Whispers from on High
Poems and short stories

Fireside Stories – With Wendy Brown
Australian Family Tales

Christmas Journeys – A Trilogy
3 Stories of Love and Family, spanning across the decades.

Coming soon:

You're
Healing Broken Hearts in Huntersville
A collection of short stories featuring the broken hearted, and God's healing presence, in the small town of Huntersville

Follow Helen Brown on:
Facebook: https://www.facebook.com/HelenBrownCollection/

Instagram: https://www.instagram.com/helen_brown_books/

Pinterest: https://www.pinterest.com.au/helenbrown58726/

Connect with Reading Stones for other great reads:
https://www.facebook.com/Reading-Stones-Publishing-and-Editing-Services-252366958298920